The author spent the later years of his professional life as a surveyor in writing survey reports, proofs of evidence and other such documents where humour is not allowed in any circumstances. Even as an examiner on the subject of building construction, all must be kept serious. It is hardly surprising, therefore, that upon retirement he was anxious to write with a freedom hitherto denied to him and this story is the consequence of that relief.

Ivor Kemp

# A SEATING OF MOLES

AUSTIN MACAULEY PUBLISHERS™

LONDON • CAMBRIDGE • NEW YORK • SHARJAH

A CIP catalogue record for this title is available from the British Library.

ISBN 9781398401358 (Paperback)
ISBN 9781788238229 (Hardback)
ISBN 9781398434011 (ePub e-book)

www.austinmacauley.com

First Published (2021)
Austin Macauley Publishers Ltd
25 Canada Square
Canary Wharf
London
E14 5LQ

The author, in advancing years, wants to thank the younger members of his family for their invaluable assistance in managing computers and comprehending signs like paper clips and abbreviations like PDF, which didn't exist in his business world.

# Chapter One

Elsie Mann was a good woman. She was good in the real sense of the word inasmuch as she was kind, helpful, attractive and always smartly turned out. Even in her mid-forties, she was attractive but still single because she was not the sort of person to compromise her principles and the men who had tried to enter her life had, quite simply, failed to make the grade. Sometimes she regretted that but deep down, Elsie knew that she could never find happiness in compromise.

She had a job, well a sort of job anyway, as a part time receptionist at the local hospital. Actually, it was a job share with a single mother so it only paid half a wage but her needs were small because she had inherited the bungalow that she lived in from her parents when they died. Being an enterprising sort, Elsie had managed to get other part-time work as well including a little job 'doing' for Mrs Lee. The two ladies had known each other vaguely from church so it wasn't surprising that they soon became good friends.

Mrs Lee was quite old but still with it and Elsie had gradually become more of a companion than just a home help. Once a week, she would help the old lady in and out of the bath and on Thursdays, the pair of them would go off shopping together in Elsie's little mini metro. Mrs Lee also lived in an inherited bungalow rather larger than Elsie's and in a deteriorating condition, especially the window frames which were continually going wrong. She had an arrangement with a local lad who would come and do odd repairs for her but he was rapidly coming to the conclusion that they were at the point where no more repair was possible.

The two ladies always went to church together for Sunday morning service and Elsie always imagined that the vicar, The Reverend Theodore Thornthwaite, had a special smile for her. That was probably because she was one of the parish workers and on the first Friday of every month, Elsie was rostered to clean all the church brasses. This was a task that she undertook willingly because she found it to be strangely therapeutic, not only that but there was something quite lovely in being in the church all alone in the echoing silence. Rev Thornthwaite, on the other hand, found her manner towards him a little embarrassing so he always took good care to keep his distance for fear of being misunderstood. In a moment of weakness once, at a Rotary Club lunch, Theodore had confessed to Willy Sidebottom, the local undertaker, that Elsie frightened him a little but Willy was very discreet.

It came to the point where Mrs Lee's windows were so bad that they became positively dangerous and the old lady thought it would be very nice to have some of this new double glazing except that it did seem to be so expensive. Elsie helped her to get some estimates but there was no way that she could afford £5000. This was the first time that Elsie realised that the old lady really wasn't all that well-off. "I've seen those adverts on the TV where you can borrow money for this sort of thing provided you have a house. I think I'll try one of them," she announced one day.

Elsie was horrified. "Do you really think that's wise? I hope you realise that these people actually take your bungalow as security so if you ever wanted to sell up and go into somewhere with a warden in your old age, you would be stuck."

"Well, I don't know what to do then because I just can't afford this sort of money."

Elsie was upset for her friend but ready to help if she could. "Look," she said, "I've got a bit put by for a rainy day. Why don't you let me give you the £5000 and then you can leave it to me in your will. Then if ever you want to move, you can pay me back from the proceeds of selling the bungalow and still have enough money left to get a little sheltered flat."

So it was agreed.

The work was carried out by Twinkleglaze in a most professional manner due in no small part to the lady surveyor controlling the job, a redhead with an Irish-sounding name who stood for no nonsense from the workforce. The money was due to be paid over as soon as the contract was completed so Elsie made all the arrangements with the bank and the cheque was handed over. The following day was a Thursday and the two ladies were going into town for shopping so Elsie arranged an appointment with Mr Jones, a solicitor, for Mrs Lee to make her will. As they drove into town, they were held up by police cars all over the place. It looked as if there had been an incident at the bank or something, they eventually had to detour round the back streets and arrived about twenty minutes late for the appointment. As Elsie was helping Mrs Lee out of the car, the old lady suffered a heart attack and died before an ambulance could get to her.

# Chapter Two

Ben Lanes was in what is commonly known as 'the building game', though why it should be referred to as a game is very hard to understand. It's an expression that covers practically everything from the lowliest labourer on the lump to Sir Robert Macalpine. Ben fell between these two levels, much nearer to the former than to the latter. He hadn't been too bright at school and like so many of his kind, he couldn't wait to leave, get a job and a pay packet as soon as he could. At the tender age of 15, he had become a tea boy and general dogsbody with a small firm of builders and began to learn, in a practical way, about life and jobbing building.

He learned lessons in the various building trades, bricklaying, plastering and plumbing and he became quite proficient in all of them, more efficient in fact than those who were supposed to be teaching him. He also learned that his boss was not a good businessman because he thought he could use the pub as an office with a mobile telephone as his means of keeping in touch with things. The consequence of this was that Ben and the others were often left on site unable to work through lack of materials, lack of instruction or both and at the end of every job, Ben and one or more of the others would be laid off. That was how he learned the parable of the seven fat cows to his cost because he had managed to spend all his wages at the beginning leaving him flat broke during the layoff. Thereafter, Ben took the simple precaution of putting a little aside each week in a bank account so that he wouldn't suffer the indignity of being skint every now and then.

Within three years, he could turn his hand to more or less anything and even had one or two private customers including old Mrs Lee, which provided a bit of pin money. When he wasn't at work, he was just like any other youngster, enjoying a pint with his pals but not before he had paid Mum for his keep. She was very strict on that sort of thing and made sure that she was around on pay day.

Things had been going rather badly lately and Ben's finances were in a poor state. He'd been laid off for five weeks and there was no prospect of getting laid back on again so he was very down in the dumps when he went to the bank to draw out his last few pounds. It was embarrassing to stand there at the till with everyone watching while the pretty cashier had to go and check something, a sure sign that she wanted to be sure that it was safe to give him the money. "It's only a miserable ten quid," he muttered as she left him standing listening to some pompous old gent making arrangements to collect £5000 in cash on the following day.

"I need it for an anonymous donation to the church roof fund," he boasted.

Ben couldn't for the life of him understand why he was cracking on about it in public if it was to be anonymous – it would serve him right if somebody gave the game away. But he finally got his ten pounds and on the way home, bought himself a well-earned pint then he gave £5 to his mother for his keep which left him with £2.97, all the money that he possessed in the whole world after more than three years of hard graft. There was nothing else for it – tomorrow he would have to go to town and sign on the dole.

The following day was a Thursday and breakfast at home had not been congenial. Ben was not in a good mood at all and his mother was at odds with the world in general. He would have liked to sit down and talk things over with her but he knew what she would say, "It's no good asking me what you should do. You chose to go into building instead of taking that job at the pub that you could have had."

So after breakfast, he set off on the long walk into town with his head down and his eyes on the pavement. As he was passing the bank, the old gent with his anonymous donation emerged tucking a brown envelope into his inside pocket. He actually collided with Ben putting him a little off balance. In that instant, Ben felt a surge of injustice and for a reason which he would never be able to explain, he just grabbed the envelope and ran. In doing so, the old gent lost his balance completely and fell to the ground cutting his head in the process. Ben simply ran as fast as he could up the side of the church, across the supermarket car park and then slowed down to a saunter as it dawned upon him that he had just committed an awful crime.

Ben wandered around for over an hour wondering what on earth to do. Part of him wanted to go to the police and own up to everything but another part of him feared the consequences of that. He was certain that the old gent had not seen his face and there had been nobody else in view when he made the snatch so Ben figured that that he had got away with it and having got away with it, he thought it best to stay away with it. The main thing to Ben was that he should get that

£5000 to its rightful place and he couldn't very well do that until the excitement had died down so he decided to hide the package for the time being. He knew that old Mrs Lee always went shopping on Thursday so he made his way over there, looked under the plant pot for her spare key and let himself in. He took a chair from the kitchen into the hall, lifted the trap door and slipped the package under loft insulating felt and quietly let himself out. When he got home, the police were waiting for him. Ben had been filmed on at least three CCTV cameras, identified and located in quick time. He was arrested.

Ben was remanded in custody. His mother disowned him and the man that she lived with, who may or may not have been his father, condemned him. Even if bail had been granted, there was not a soul able or willing to post it so he was put into a remand prison where he encountered some of the worst lowlifes imaginable. Ben had met some rough types in the building game but they had nothing on this lot. His only visit was from the solicitor appointed to defend him and he was not exactly encouraging. "What can we say in your defence?" he asked. Ben came right out with the truth.

"Probably nothing," he said. "The fact is that I just had a mad moment; I don't know what came over me and I regretted my action as soon as I had committed it."

"According to the police, they have evidence that you were in the bank at the same time as the victim on the day before the crime so you knew that he would be collecting the money next day therefore you laid in wait for him. That seems pretty damning to me. I expect you'll go down for this."

"Is there nothing I can do?" pleaded Ben.

"Yes – tell the Police where you hid the money and plead guilty. You might get a shorter stretch then." And that was the end of that interview.

Back in the cell, Ben was pretty fed up and a cellmate was doing his best to help.

"I've been advised to say where I hid the money and plead guilty," Ben told the helpful fellow. "Whatever you do, don't say where the money is or else the cops will go and nick it for themselves. Then you'll get done for wasting police time as well. It happened to me first time."

"Oh! Surely not," said Ben, "someone must have discovered it first."

"Don't you believe it, mate. That money was too well hidden for that. It could only have been the cops."

Ben weighed this advice very carefully before deciding to keep his own counsel. It was utterly paramount to Ben's future that this money should get to the church where it belonged and the only way he could be certain of that was to serve his sentence then retrieve the money when he got out so that he could take it to where it belonged.

The trial was short. He got two years.

# Chapter Three

Elsie Mann left it a decent two weeks after the funeral before enquiring about her £5000. Mr Jones, the solicitor, had been ever so considerate and helpful when old Mrs Lee had died on his doorstep and had even arranged the funeral. That was a very simple affair because, it transpired, that the old lady had had no surviving relatives. Elsie had offered to help but the solicitor rather took over so far as the actual arrangements were concerned. The funeral had been delayed because there had been an inquest, something to do with the fact that the old lady hadn't been under the doctor for anything when she died – Elsie didn't really understand. But now the solicitor had told her that he was unable to let her have the £5000.

Somewhat in desperation, she went to see Reverend Thornthwaite to see if he could find out how long she would have to wait because she depended on her little bit of interest and the bit of wages that Mrs Lee had given her to run her little car. Theodore had not looked forward to the meeting. Elsie was obviously upset at the recent loss of a friend as well as concerned about losing her money but somehow he couldn't quite bring himself to give the warm sympathy that she clearly needed because he was afraid that it might be misunderstood. He promised to have a word with Jones on the following Monday when he went to the Rotary Club lunch but it would have to be off the record. Elsie understood and thanked him, perhaps a little too warmly, for his help.

Alan Jones was a good solicitor, one of the old school ones who did everything correctly. Nevertheless, he could well understand the predicament of Elsie so he was hardly surprised when Theodore raised the matter at lunch on Monday. "This is a very difficult case so far as your friend is concerned," he began.

Theodore interrupted, "Not exactly a friend, you understand, but a parishioner."

"Whatever you say," replied Jones, "but the thing is the old lady died intestate as far as we can make out and there seems to be no way that she will get her money now. If the old lady had any surviving relatives, we could make an appeal there but I'm expecting the public trustee to send me instructions to get the place sold and the proceeds will, according to the law, revert to the crown. They will have no dispensation to make any exception."

"I rather feared that might be the case," said Theodore already beginning to fear having to convey such terrible news to poor Elsie. But he wouldn't shirk his duty so after the Rotary Club meeting, he went straight round to Elsie's and explained that she wouldn't get her £5000 back. She was distraught.

"Of course, I'll have to sell my car and go back to cycling," she declared after getting over the initial shock.

Theodore felt inadequate. "Something will come up, you see if it doesn't," then added lamely, "The Lord will provide."

Elsie gave him one of her warm smiles as he left and thanked him for being so honest about it. What else could I have been, he thought as he walked backwards down the path hoping that Elsie would go indoors and not wave him down the road.

# Chapter Four

Vic Spooner was another one in what is commonly called the building game. He was positioned somewhere between Ben Lanes and Sir Robert Macalpine, although Vic would probably have referred to the latter as Sir Albert MacRockpine because Vic had a quirk. Very much like his august Reverend namesake, Vic had a way of sometimes getting his words a bit muddled, most noticeably when he was worried or excited. Because of these spoonerisms, he was occasionally referred to as Rev rather than Vic but that didn't worry him in the least. He was a humorous, good-natured soul who had inherited from his father a one-man business doing unambitious jobbing building works about the town but Vic had built it up from those small beginnings into a comparative empire boasting a workforce of four jacks-of-all-trades, an office, a yard and a very pretty secretary who doubled as a loving daughter.

Vic had been brought up 'on the tools' as they say in the trade so most of the week, he was in his overalls turning his hand to anything that needed to be done and that often included plain hard labouring. But on Mondays, he went to the office wearing a suit because that was the day that the Rotary Club would meet for lunch in a modest but satisfactory hotel in town. This was Vic's day for drumming up business promotion – call it what you will but Vic had to admit that he enjoyed it. It was really an association of local trade and business people but more than that because the club was forever raising funds or offering material help to local charities and in a significant way, the Rotary Club benefited the town. Like any other club, Rotary had its rules and one important rule was that only one member for each trade or profession was allowed thus there was one banker, one solicitor and in this case, one minister of religion. Vic was lucky to be in the club at all and it was only because somebody was a little elastic with the rules as a means of boosting the membership. So, whereas John Carruthers of Carruthers Brothers was listed as 'Building Contractor', Vic Spooner was listed as 'Building Repairs'. It was fine in theory but the two men were in competition for business and it frequently showed in their behaviour to one another.

Another of Rotary's little tricks was to call some older members 'Senior Active', which enabled them to release a category for a new member without requiring the older man to leave. But, all in all, it was a good club which did good work as well as providing a medium for the sort of information that Theodore had managed to glean for Elsie Mann.

The town council had a most refreshing way of dealing with necessary local matters. Empire building was positively discouraged in every department. Chief officers were required to employ only sufficient staff to enable them to ensure that the council's obligations were discharged efficiently and where there were trades or professions in town to undertake council contracts, then they should be engaged rather than the council employing people direct. Thus David Thorburn, a chartered surveyor, having been elected to the council's list of approved contractors, would find himself instructed, from time to time, to act upon council's behalf in some capacity.

John Carruthers was on the approved list of building contractors but Vic Spooner was not and that was a bone of contention. The two men did not get on well at the best of times and were often found in red faced conversation just short of confrontation which was a source of some amusement to other members of the Rotary Club. What rankled most with Vic was the fact that Carruthers could get the occasional contract from the council to repair or renovate council property which Vic knew very well could have been done less expensively by his own firm and to get onto that coveted list, you had first to complete two or three large contracts on time and within budget so that the borough architect could look at them and make a judgement. Poor old Vic had had misfortune in that department because the last two major jobs he had undertaken had ended up with a bankrupt client owing him lots of money which was irrecoverable. And that wasn't the end of it because his working capital had been drained and the bank was far from helpful.

Vic had seen Simpson, the bank manager, at Rotary lunch but he was faced with a stone wall when it came to favours. "I'll put up the same amount as you put up," was all he would say so somehow Vic had got to get hold of hard cash as well as good quality work. Carruthers ribbed him unmercifully as a jobbing builder who only needed a few bob in his back pocket which was why they were red faced today.

David Thorburn was sympathetic of Vic's position and tried to help. He came over to the arguing pair and said,

"When you two have finished your fight, I'd like a word with you, Vic." This made Carruthers angrier than ever until Jones the solicitor came over and broke it up with his usual sense of humour.

"I'll see you two in court one of these days if you don't stop your arguing. It could become a famous case – Spooner v Carruthers brothers and others. It'll get into all the text books just because of the name." Everyone laughed and the tension passed.

It was on the following Thursday that Vic came into the office and took the mail from Penny who had been in for half an hour already. Vic had always wanted a son to follow him into the business but things simply hadn't worked out that way but Penny had turned up trumps. She managed the office and the men expertly, did all the wages and accounts and had even taught herself to write a specification as well as any architect he knew. Vic soon cast aside the bills and humphed and took into his office only the big fat envelope which he had been expecting from David Thorburn. It contained a plan and specification of some improvement works to a bungalow with an invitation to tender for the works. Vic was far from certain that he would be able to carry the initial expense of progressing the work to the first interim payment but he would have to try. He called out from the office.

"Penny love! Get on to these surveyors and find out what they are doing about payments, will you?"

"OK, Dad."

She was back in a few minutes with the information he wanted. "He says his client has just bought this place and he wants it all ready for when he gets back from abroad. He says that he has access to all the money needed and is authorised to pay you in monthly instalments. I asked him to make it fortnightly but he says that isn't possible."

"Thanks for trying anyway, but I'm going to put a price in anyway and just hope I can wangle some credit from suppliers."

As she went out of the office, Penny called back, "Isn't that the bungalow that old Mrs Lee used to live in before she died?"

"I do believe it is, now that you mention it. Didn't your mother know her at the WI?"

"Yes, that's right. She died without making her will or something so as she had no surviving relations, all her property goes to the crown."

"That doesn't seem very fair," said Vic with feeling. "I'd have thought she had enough of her own."

So with some concern, Vic went along the following day to measure up and do his estimating. *At least,* he thought, *if I can't do the job for lack of funds, I can make sure that young Thorburn gets a fair price in his file.* It might just make his client think twice about the payments only being monthly.

The alterations included building an extra bedroom and a bathroom in the loft so Vic was armed with ladder and torch so that he could properly work out how the job could be done. It was as he was coming out of the loft that Vic lost his balance, reached out to steady himself and landed on his backside in the hall feeling very foolish indeed. He had dragged with him a couple of yards of insulating quilt and with it something more solid. It was a packet of money; there must have been about £5000 in there, thought Vic.

He sat on the floor for a long time, pondering. On the one hand, it wasn't his but on the other hand, nobody would know if he kept it. On the one hand, £5000 would make no difference to the crown, whoever that might be, but on the other hand, it was just the sort of cash Vic needed to get back on his feet. He reasoned that it must have been put there by old Mrs Lee rather than the new owner. All in all, it would be better all-round if he just hung on to it. So he did.

Next day, he submitted his estimate then cut along to the bank where he put the cash on the manager's desk with a grand flourish and received an assurance that he could run up an overdraft of a like amount on the bungalow job. Funnily enough, the bank manager seemed genuinely pleased to help a Rotary Club colleague and wished him luck.

Vic won the contract to improve and repair the bungalow. He worked very hard on it and brought it to completion two weeks within the contract term. He earned a profit of £8000. David Thorburn was sufficiently impressed to give him another chance which was another success and made him another £10000 profit. His application to be placed upon the council's list of Approved contractors was accepted and Vic thought that, at last, he had made it. He could now look forward to quality work with a fair paymaster who would not go broke at the critical moment. He could also face Carruthers at Rotary on equal terms.

On the following Monday, he went to the meeting in high spirits and couldn't wait to rub salt into the Carruthers wound and said to nobody in particular but so that everyone could hear, "Now that I'm on the council's list, I need more staff – what I need is a damn good clerk of works to deal with all the extra work." Phil Collins (estate agency) overheard this remark, not surprisingly, and came over to Vic.

"Did I hear you say you wanted a clerk of works? If so, I know of a chap who might suit you. He's working with a big firm at the moment but I'm sure he'd prefer to be more autonomous in a smaller concern. Should I put him in touch?"

"By all means," replied Vic. "I much prefer a pre-commendation." Collins was used to Vic's funny words and made no remark.

"In that case, I'll give him your address. His name is Len Baynes."

"Len Baynes," Vic repeated so as to memorise it. "I'll look forward to seeing him."

Then the bell went and they all filed in to lunch. That day, Vic sang grace with more volume than usual.

# Chapter Five

Ben came out of prison after 15 months. He had been a model prisoner who had managed to keep himself to himself because his size and strength had kept him free from the usual prison bullies. Those 15 months had turned him into a man, a real man, with a grim determination to make a better job of the rest of his life and quite definitely to keep out of the sort of trouble that gets a man back into prison. He had made good use of his time inside with a bit of studying. He found a couple of books about quantity surveying in the prison library that nobody else wanted to borrow so had more or less kept them as his own until his release. Fellow prisoners thought he was mad for reading such tripe but when one of them asked why, Ben looked up and snarled a reply, "Haven't you noticed that all the rich criminals are smart ones. Daft criminals like you just spend your time in and out of prison and finish up with nothing – just like you will." That served to keep other enquirers at a distance.

The prisoners aid people had fixed him up with accommodation in a hostel because he couldn't go home. He would have been thrown out on his ear for sure. The first thing to do was to retrieve the stolen money so he decided to go to see Mrs Lee, make a clean breast of the whole incident and ask for her help in getting the money back to the church roof fund. When he got there, his heart dropped. This was clearly no longer Mrs Lee's bungalow. It had been renovated and of far more concern to Ben was the fact that there was obviously a new room in the loft so surely somebody had had discovered his haul and no doubt made off with it. Ben knocked at the door with a heavy heart but there was no reply. He knocked next door and soon learned that Mrs Lee had died suddenly just over a year ago. "It was very sad really. She was on the way to see her solicitor to make a will and she died on his doorstep."

"Oh dear!" was Ben's inadequate reply.

So there he was without a job and without the stolen money. He would have to get a job but he knew that wasn't going to be easy especially as his address at the hostel would give away his past. Even so, he must try so he made a list of all the builders he had ever come into contact with before he became a criminal and set about going round to every one of them to try and get work.

There were several brush offs and a lot of disappointment in the next two days. Then he arrived at the splendid offices of Carruthers Brothers High Class Building Contractors. *Fat chance here,* thought Ben, *with their fancy name and title,* but he did get in to see John Carruthers in person.

As soon as it came out that Ben was in a hostel, Carruthers asked, "Have you got a criminal record by any chance?"

"As a matter of fact I have," said Ben feeling despondent, "but I've put all that behind me and I promise that I'll never go back to a life of crime. I just need a chance to get started that's all."

"Well, I tell you what," said a helpful-sounding Carruthers, "I happen to know that my good friend Vic Spooner is looking for a clerk of works. Why don't you go round and see him."

This was more encouraging than anything that Ben had turned up so far so off he went at the double.

After Ben had gone, Carruthers turned to his secretary and remarked, "You know, I think old Spooner is just daft enough to employ a jailbird. That should soon get him back to jobbing building where he belongs."

Vic sat in his office rather less sure of himself than usual. He had never really employed anyone of importance before, usually hiring tradesmen that he had known on and off beforehand but now that he had actually shown his hand, he would have to deliver or lose face. Penny was in the outer office, busy behind her desk with its telephone and typewriter. Vic called out, "Penny love, come in a minute and we'll try and do an advert for the paper." Penny did everything properly and went in with notebook at the ready. "What do you think we ought to say," queried Vic as she sat down.

"Well, we ought to ask for someone with experience, old enough to command the respect of the workforce and the right sort of background," she began.

This wasn't going to be easy, Vic was thinking when they heard somebody come into the outer office. Penny got up and went to see who it was. Vic heard the conversation.

"Hello, can I be of help?"

"I hope so. I've come about the clerk of works job. A very good friend of Mr Spooner sent me along."

"Just a moment, Sir, I'll see if Mr Spooner is free to see you."

Penny came back in with a very broad smile on her face. Vic thought, *She obviously likes the look of him – it must be the fellow that Collins told me about.*

He said, "I've been expecting this chap, someone at Rotary told me about him. Does he look alright?"

Penny flushed just a hint, "He looks fine to me, Daddy. Shall I send him in?"

"Yes love. I'd better do a proper interview."

Which is exactly what Vic didn't do because he had no idea how to. "What's your name, young man?"

"Ben Lanes," he replied.

It had a familiar ring to it. "Well, young Baynes; you come highly recommended. I understand you have a background in the building game and you are looking for something a bit better. Is that right?"

Ben was a little confused but assumed that Vic had misheard the name.

"Well yes, I'm certainly looking for something better and I'm prepared to work hard to get it."

This was said with such conviction that Vic was almost prepared to give him the job there and then but pulled himself up in time to at least appear to be going through the right motions, whatever they were. "Perhaps you can tell me a bit about your background."

Ben gave a detailed account of the trades he had learned and then surprised Vic by displaying a working knowledge of quantity surveying, a very useful adjunct.

"Well, Baynes, you look OK to me but I need a little time to consider. Would you mind waiting outside."

Ben thought that this was where he got the old heave-ho but at least they hadn't asked his address yet. Still, he might

29

get that wrong with any luck, after all the old man couldn't seem to get his name right.

Ben went to the outer office to be greeted by a warm smile from the very pretty receptionist. He stood wondering what to do and feeling very much as if the girl was staring at him so he pretended to look out of the window. Vic's voice called out, "Penny love, come in a minute please to consult."

She replied, "Coming, Daddy," which told Ben something that he had started to guess anyway because there was a family likeness. As Penny went through, she looked back at Ben and said, somewhat uselessly, "Do take a seat."

Ben looked around but the only seat in the room was Penny's behind the desk so he did as he was told and sat in it. The door closed on Penny and Vic leaving Ben wondering what would happen.

As he sat there looking more like a clerk than an applicant for a job, another chap came in, older than Ben and clearly experienced by the way he looked critically around. He stood in front of Ben and said, "I'm told that there's a sort of job going here and I've come about it. Name of Baynes, Len Baynes."

Ben took in the mistake in a flash and realised what had happened but he wasn't to be beaten so near the post. Anyway, this Chap's attitude was wrong. "Sorry," he said, "post's already been filled."

"Can't say I'm sorry," said the other. "Doesn't look much of a firm anyway so I wouldn't want to give up my present job for this." And with that he left.

Penny came out all smiles. "Daddy will see you now," she said. Ben went back in and sat down.

"I've decided to give you a try, lad. I must say I was hoping to get someone a little older but we both think you can fit in nicely here." Vic held out his hand and said, "Welcome to the firm. How soon can you start?"

"As soon as you like. Will tomorrow be OK?"

"Certainly. Now I've got things to do so would you mind giving all your details to Penny. She's my daughter you know – does all the business and leaves the building to me."

Ben knew that the next bit was going to be the difficult bit. As soon as he gave his address and national insurance details to Penny, she would know that he'd been inside and that would be that. But he hadn't taken into account the fact that Penny liked him and already was looking forward to having a good-looking young man about the office for a change. Ben decided to come clean so he told Penny right out where he had been for the last 15 months. "I ought to have told your father but I've suffered so many disappointments," he trailed off lamely.

Penny thought about it for a while, feeling a little disappointment herself. "Of course, Daddy must be told," she said, "but I think he is likely to be very busy for the next two weeks so I'll not have a chance until then. If, in the meantime, he has come to rely on you a bit, there's always a chance that he'll turn a blind eye. It's up to you."

Ben could hardly believe his luck. "Miss, I can't tell you how much I appreciate the chance you are taking and I'll do my utmost to make sure that you never regret it."

"Never?" She looked up at him. "That is a long time, oh! And another thing. If you are going to work here, you call me Penny, not Miss." They both smiled and as Ben left, he felt like leaping in the air for joy. A chance was all he needed.

Over the next two weeks, Ben worked so hard. He read up the file notes of every job on site. He went around every job and introduced himself to the workforce and gained their confidence by asking them whether there were any problems that he could iron out. He very soon made certain that the men were never left idle through waiting for materials or precise instructions and soon had every man on the workforce doing a full eight hours a day rather than seven hours working and one hanging about. He was first in every morning and last out in the evening so by the time Vic found out about his murky past, Ben had become a reliable and valuable asset. Vic said, "You could have told me, Len. I would have understood."

"Ben," the young man corrected.

"Eh?"

"It's Ben, not Len."

"Yes, of course."

There was no doubt that Vic's business was on the up and up. The council had sent through a job, admittedly modest, but he could understand that. Ben gave it his very closest attention and was properly deferential to the council officers. When the job was completed, they expressed their satisfaction to Vic and paid tribute to Ben's helpful attitude. Other jobs started coming in and Ben found Penny to be a very helpful and clever young woman. Whenever a contract came in with a penalty clause for taking too long, Penny would ask for and usually get a bonus clause for finishing early. Then Ben would tell the men and make sure that the bonus was paid to them, not to the firm. So they all worked harder and more cheerfully so that gradually Vic's firm built up a reputation for good quality work delivered on time.

Ben soon managed to move out of the hostel into proper digs and started to see Penny socially as well as at work. They enjoyed each other's company very much but tended to keep their liaison rather quiet because neither knew quite how Mr and Mrs Spooner might react to their little girl going out with an ex-con. Ben was saving hard so they didn't go out on expensive dates. Ben wouldn't be free to spend freely until he had repaid his debt to the church roof fund and he might have to explain that to Penny before long but not just yet.

Vic was in his element and prone to crow about how well the firm was doing. At Rotary Club, he was rubbing it in a bit with Carruthers who was not best pleased to be losing good contracts to what he still referred to as a jobbing builder. "I can't believe you are doing that well just because you've employed a jailbird. You'd better watch out or he'll start robbing you, you know."

"How did you know he'd been inside? I've certainly never told anyone."

"As it happens, he came to me first so I sent him round to you because your work is closer to breaking stones than the quality work that I get."

Vic was furious and about to launch into a tirade about fair dealing when Jones butted in. "Don't you two ever stop arguing for a second? Now come on through because the bell has gone for lunch, not for round one."

They went in and made sure that they sat as far apart as they could.

As the weeks went by, Mrs Spooner noticed that Ben and Penny were becoming quite involved in their relationship but Vic was far too busy and lacking in perception to notice that anything was going on at all. An exceptionally large package of plans and specifications had arrived from the town hall with an invitation to tender for converting six old houses into twenty-four flats and Vic was immersed in quantities and pricings because he really wanted this job. He called Ben in and consulted over timing, method and staff requirements so that he could be as competitive as possible whilst remaining on the right side of profit. Tenders had to be in by 10 a.m. on the Friday morning and they were all to be opened at 10.30 with contractors invited to be present when the council's architect read them all out and announced the result. Vic went along and so did John Carruthers.

"What are you doing here? This is a bit out of your league, isn't it, or perhaps you like to come along and watch."

Vic bridled at the slur. "I'm here because I expect to win, so don't be too sure of yourself."

The tenders were read out and Vic was the lowest by the tightest of margins. He couldn't be bothered to insult Carruthers but rushed off back to the office. "Penny love, we've made it. This is our first million-pound contract. We ought to celebrate – what do you say?"

Mrs Spooner had been shopping and had popped into the office on the way home to find out the result of the tender and she was pleased as the others. She popped out from the office behind Vic and made him jump. "What is the best restaurant in town?" she enquired. "I think you ought to push the boat out on Saturday because it's Penny's birthday as well. Oh! And I think you might invite young Ben along as well because he has been partly responsible for your recent success, don't you think?"

"Hello love, what a surprise seeing you here. But you are absolutely right. If you make a booking for 8 o'clock, I'll speak to Len and tell him to wear his best suit."

Penny said, "Do you mind if I tell Ben?" emphasising the B, "I'd love to see his face."

Vic sensed something in the way that Penny said that which he couldn't quite identify. "OK. Love. You tell him. And say we'll pick him up at ten to eight."

Whether or not the dinner party was a success depends upon your point of view. Mrs Spooner booked a table at the Majestic and it turned out to be every bit as good as people had said it would be. There was a maitre d' and a wine waiter as well as all the other little French- or Italian-sounding fellows who could constantly be seen emerging backwards through a padded green door with prodigious amounts of food and crockery balanced on hands and forearms as only skilled waiters are able to do. Vic drew the wine waiter aside and gave him a significant gratuity for appearing at his signal with a celebratory bottle of champagne at the end of the meal and then they all took their seats with a drink in hand. The meal was great, no two ways about it. And the conversation and laughter were enjoyable as well. The wine flowed, especially down Vic's throat and the whole party was in mellow mood when, with coffee served, Vic stood up to make his little speech.

"Today is Penny's twenty first birthday and I am proud to have her here with us today. It cannot have escaped many people that a builder should be blessed with a son to do his donkey work but I can say with conviction that our Penny has turned out to be as much as, if not more than any son could be. She is a mainstay of the business and your mother and me are as proud as punch. This is a very special day which calls for champagne," and so saying, he raised his right hand and snapped his fingers whereupon the wine waiter stepped forward deferentially and proffered a bottle of wine for Vic's inspection and approval.

"Just a minute," interrupted Penny. The wine waiter withdrew with the bottle unopened. "There's something else to celebrate as well. Today Ben asked me to marry him and I have accepted and we are both very happy indeed."

Vic looked a little surprised at this but when he glanced at Mrs Spooner, he could tell that she already had an inkling that this might happen and was happy about it so Vic beamed as well.

"Well I never," declared Vic. "This really is fantastic news." All the time thinking what an advantage it would be to have the firm's best assistant tied to the business by marriage. "This really does call for Champagne," whereat he again raised his right hand and snapped his fingers. Once more the wine waiter stepped forward with the champagne and held it for Vic's approval.

"Just a minute," said Ben. The wine waiter stepped back with a sigh. "Before you all celebrate too much, there is something that I want to get off my chest. It is no secret to this family that my past has a shadow and I'm truly grateful that none of you have ever asked how it was that I went to prison. The thing is that I want to make a clean breast of it before I become part of the family. I knocked an old man down in the street and stole £5000 from him. What makes it worse is that I knew that he intended that money to be an anonymous donation to the church roof fund. I've regretted my action ever since and I promise you all that I will never again turn to crime. But it is important to Penny especially that all my savings will be put to replacing that money so it will be a long time before I can afford to be married."

He sat down to silence from Mr And Mrs, Spooner but Penny was smiling broadly because she knew it was the right thing to do.

Vic broke the silence. "I'm glad you told us, Len, but why didn't you just give back the money that you had stolen then you wouldn't be having to save up now."

"I lost it."

"How did you manage to lose five grand?"

Ben explained how he had wandered the streets and decided to hide the money in a loft because he was afraid to take it home.

"Well, if it's still there," said Vic, "can't we find a way to retrieve it?"

"Well, no," said Ben. "You see the bungalow has changed hands and the new owners have turned the loft into a bedroom."

Vic was starting to redden and Penny was becoming suspicious. "Would this be a bungalow in Bradbury Street?" she enquired.

"Actually, it was." Ben wondered how she could have guessed.

"The one Mrs Lee used to live in?"

"Well yes. It was that one actually."

Penny looked accusingly at her father. "You found that money, didn't you? I thought at the time that you were up against it financially yet you managed to carry that job along."

Vic was very embarrassed now. "Since you raise the matter, I did stumble across a packet of money at that place so I put it to good use. What's wrong with that?"

"You stole it, Daddy, that's what's wrong with it."

"Well, he stole it first," now on his feet and pointing the accusing finger at Ben.

Now Ben was on his feet too. "I didn't do 15 months in prison so that you could carry a job along."

It was time for Mrs Spooner to interpose. "Sit down the pair of you and just behave yourselves. Can't you see that everyone in the place is looking at you."

The two men sat down shamefacedly. Mrs Spooner carried on in a more conciliatory tone. "Since you have both stolen the money on separate occasions, I suggest you share the money and the shame. It is no secret, Vic, that you are not getting any younger and you are going to need Ben more and more. So as he is coming into the family, why don't you take him into the partnership as well. That £5000 is now part of the working capital of the business so as partners, you can make equal use of it."

The two men eyed each other across the table and both quietly nodded assent. "I agree to that," said Vic.

"Aye, and so do I," returned Ben.

"Well, thank goodness for that." Mrs Spooner brought the subject to a close.

"This calls for champagne," said Vic as he raised his right hand and snapped his fingers. The wine waiter stepped forward once again with a bottle of champagne and a sigh.

"Just a minute," it was Penny again. "I'm not happy to have a fiancé and a father trading with stolen money especially as the firm is now in a fit state to repay that money to its rightful place so the marriage is off unless you find a way between you of making sure that the anonymous donation gets to its proper place within seven days. Is that clear."

Both men felt that they would rest easier when that had been done.

"I agree to that."

"And so do I. This calls for champagne," and Vic raised his right hand and snapped his fingers but the wine waiter had gone.

"Oh, stop calling for the bloody stuff and get it poured," said Mrs Spooner. The other diners all sighed. Vic looked behind him and saw that the wine waiter had left it in an ice bucket so, having had quite a few already, he reached unsteadily for the bottle, almost overbalanced but saved himself at the expense of shaking the bottle rather more than he ought to have done. He untwisted the wire and eased the cork until it fired out of the bottle straight towards the green padded door where the waiters emerged just as Alphonse was coming out laden with dishes of sticky toffee something or other for table nine. Alphonse sensed, rather than saw, the missile coming straight at him so he stopped, wound his neck down a couple of millimetres and the cork smacked harmlessly into the woodwork just above his head. But in pausing, instead of clearing the doorway, Alphonse had committed the cardinal sin of all waiters. As he stepped away with his right foot, the door slammed into his left heel and stopped suddenly so that Enrique, following close behind backside first and similarly laden, came to a full stop with his back and elbows against the inside of the door whilst the plates and contents continued their forward rush into

Enrique's midriff. As Alphonse stepped away with his left foot, thereby leaving the door free to swing again, Enrique was totally off balance so came staggering out backwards apace until he finally fell against the back of Alphonse's knees causing him to pitch headlong towards table nine delivering the hot sticky something-or-others onto the table from about a yard away.

In the ensuing melee, Vic raised his glass in a toast. "To the prosperity of Spooner and Baynes," he declared.

"Lanes."

"Eh?"

"Lanes. My name is Lanes not Baynes."

"Oh, sorry lad. To Looner and Spains," he tried again but the others had by then given up. They raised their glasses and their eyes towards Heaven, each with their own thoughts.

Penny thought, *Poor Daddy, he does get in such a muddle sometimes.*

Ben thought, *So long as the lawyers get it right on the partnership deed.*

And Mrs Spooner thought, *Silly old bugger's losing his marbles.*

And they drank to the success of the new firm whatever it was going to be called.

# Chapter Six

Vic could hardly wait for Rotary lunch on Monday so that he could crow about his success. He arrived early and saw in the bar that Carruthers was nursing a gin and tonic, Phil. Collins, the estate agent, was in conversation with Willy Sidebottom the undertaker and Arthur Simpson from the bank was sitting alone reading Bankers' Weekly. Vic went straight towards Simpson who folded his magazine and greeted Vic, "Hello, old chap. How's my investment in your business."

Vic replied loudly enough for all to hear, "Very well actually. I've just landed my first million-pound contract and I've taken on a new partner as well." Vic was pleased to see Carruthers splutter into his glass at the news.

"Anyone I know?" asked the banker.

"You might do – a young fellow called Baynes. Knows the business well and a damn good worker. He's going to make a big difference to me, you know."

Collins, overhearing this, remarked to Sidebottom, "Do you know, Spooner never ceases to surprise me. It must have been a couple of years or more since I recommended Baynes. He was turned down flat at the time but now, it seems, Spooner has had a change of heart. He's a nice fellow in my opinion."

Sidebottom looked at Collins coldly and said, "I can't stand the man. He always refers to me as Silly Widebottom and I can't believe it's a mistake every time."

The bell rang and they all went in to lunch.

It wasn't until the Wednesday that Vic and Ben got around to doing anything about repaying the money. They had a discussion and agreed that Friday morning would be best. They phoned the bank and made arrangements to collect the £5000 at about 10 a.m. on Friday then they would drive to the church. Ben would go in and deposit it in a suitable place while Vic waited outside in the van. Ben was pleased that the money would be in a brown package with the bank's rubber stamp on it, just like the package he had stolen so long ago, so long in fact that the roof of the church had been repaired for over a year now. Now that the work was done, Theodore felt more comfortable in the place and had taken to going to the Vestry on a Friday morning to write his sermon for Sunday. It was quiet in the Vestry and he enjoyed the tranquillity, somehow inspiring.

Soon after 10, Ben came very quietly into the church. It was a rare visit for Ben and he was, as always, rather awestruck by the echoey silence of the place. Nobody was about, so far as he could see but that didn't prevent him from tiptoeing like a burglar. Close to the entrance he looked for a suitable place to put his bundle but there was nowhere suitable. There was a slot for 'Overseas Missions' and another for 'Books and Publications' but these slots had been designed to collect half crowns at the most and he would never be able to stuff five grand in one of those. Neither could he leave it lying about where any Tom, Dick or Harry could come in off the street and make off with it. Ben knew enough about church to be aware that the safest place would be behind the big cross on the altar because only the Vicar went up there, but he was nervous, somehow afraid to go up there himself because it was too holy. But he reasoned that his intentions were of the highest so there would be no sin in going behind the altar on this occasion.

He went very cautiously down the side aisle, not quite knowing why he avoided the bold approach down the centre. When he got there, he took the packet from his inside pocket and thought he ought to write on it that it was an anonymous donation to the church roof fund. He had a cheap ballpoint in his top pocket and started to write.

Elsie Mann rode her bicycle up to the Vestry door, unlocked it and let herself in to polish the brass. "Good morning, Vicar," she announced breezily as she saw Theodore writing his sermon.

Ben heard the voices and jumped out of his skin dropping the pen as he did so. He was petrified with fear at the prospect of being discovered here. He had only written 'An anonymous donation' but that would have to do because he had no intention of staying in church now that he knew there was somebody about. On the tips of his toes, he ran down the side aisle in a cold sweat, let himself out as quietly as he could and ran for the van where Vic was waiting. "I need a drink and quick," he said and Vic took him off to the pub where he explained his terror.

Elsie and Theodore had not heard a sound as it happened and as Elsie was getting the cleaning materials out of the cupboard, Theodore asked her, "Elsie, will you be seeing Doreen Hill in the next couple of days?"

"I don't suppose so, she comes in tomorrow to do the flowers so we don't often come into contact but I could call in if you like."

"Oh, that won't be necessary. I only wanted to remind her about the supper at the vicarage on Saturday week for all the church helpers. You'll be coming, won't you?"

"Yes Vicar, I'll be there."

"Then I'll leave Doreen a note." Theodore looked among his papers on the desk then patted all his pockets. "Oh dear, I seem to have lost my pen," he announced.

"Here, borrow mine," said Elsie and gave him a big smile because she was pleased to be of help.

"Thank you." He wrote the note and put it where Doreen couldn't miss it then turned to Elsie. "I've finished here now so I'll leave by the front door and lock up behind me then you can lock the Vestry when you go. Will that be alright?"

"That'll be fine," chirped Elsie. "Cheerio."

When Theodore had gone, Elsie wallowed in the delightful silence of the church which she enjoyed so much then went about her polishing, beginning, as she always did, with the big cross. As she stepped up to it, she trod on something which splintered under her foot. She looked down and saw a broken ballpoint pen. "The vicar must have dropped it," she muttered to herself. Then she saw the brown package labelled 'An anonymous donation'. Elsie picked up the package carefully wondering what it was. She began to entertain the strangest thoughts as she pulled open one end and found money – lots of it. It didn't take long to estimate that it was £5000, precisely the amount she had lost in trying to help Mrs Lee. And hadn't Theodore told her that the Lord would provide! Surely this was Theodore's way of helping

44

her – it must be – all the hints were there, the pen and all that stuff about writing a note for Doreen. No. She was certain in her mind that Theodore had left this money for her but in such a way that it would have to remain a secret, their secret, not even to be mentioned by either of them to the other. What a wonderful man he was.

A week later, when Elsie arrived at the vicarage for supper with all the other helpers, she came not on her bicycle but in her new, used, Mini Metro. She gave Theodore a warm, knowing smile. He wondered why and asked himself for the hundredth time what that woman was up to.

# Chapter Seven

The change in Elsie Mann didn't go unnoticed at the WI. For so long she had appeared to be morose and unhappy, and who could blame her. She had suffered a cruel fate when Mrs Lee had died so suddenly as the members had heard so many times but in spite of that, she had a lot of sympathy. Now she was smiling once again like her old self and Mrs Spooner had to admit that the light in her face made her look a very attractive woman once more. Perhaps it was rude of the others to talk about Elsie behind her back but they did and they all agreed that it wasn't just because she had her car back. Oh no! This was the demeanour of a woman in love. The tongues would wag and Elsie knew it but her secret remained well and truly kept. It had to. She contented herself with carefully folding and wrapping the empty brown paper package amongst her treasures. This was to her an emblem, a token which she could cherish all her life.

# Chapter Eight

Briony Freshwater was born of an Irish mother and a father about whom she knew nothing but his name. By the time she was 16, she had grown into a very attractive girl with long blonde hair and a figure that would cause men to turn their heads and the boys to whistle and without being unduly extrovert, she quietly enjoyed the attention. She was quite clever with her school work and left with a couple of good A levels and another not so good. Perhaps she could have gone to university but that was not for Briony. She had never wanted to be anything but a nurse and with those qualifications, she was accepted into nursing college gladly. There she devoted herself to work and study and eventually came out as a full-fledged nurse, eager to take on the job at the sharp end.

But like so many like her, whilst she was willing and hardworking, she was not so good at managing her finances. Heaven knows, the pay for a junior nurse wasn't good but Briony's expectations were not unlike those of any young woman of comparable age earning much more. As a newly qualified person, she was bombarded with offers of cheap loans, credit cards and more so, it was very easy to overspend and find herself with a mounting debt problem which simply could not be met from her pay. She shared a little flat with another nurse, seven years her senior, and because of the awkward hours, had found it desirable to have a little car. She needed help.

Beryl, the flatmate, came home from duty to find Briony in an obvious state of agitation. She asked, "Whatever is making you so long faced?"

Briony hardly knew where to begin but she was pretty desperate for help and advice from someone and Beryl was that much older and more experienced so she felt able to confide. "The truth is, I'm spending more than I earn and yet I don't really do anything extravagant. Unless something happens soon, I'm afraid I shall have to give up the car and go back to riding a bike but I really don't fancy late nights and early mornings around this neighbourhood without a big male chaperone if there is such a thing."

Beryl was sympathetic because she had been there and done it herself. "When I was on junior's pay, I managed to get a supplementary job three nights a week in a pub but I have to admit that it was very hard going. If I had had a face and a figure like yours, I would have done something far less demanding and a lot more profitable."

"I hope you don't mean what I think you mean," answered Briony with a slight flush.

"Certainly not, young lady, nothing immoral at all. I'm talking about strippagrams."

"You mean taking all your clothes off in front of a load of men?"

"Exactly."

"I couldn't do that. Anyway, isn't it dangerous?"

"Not dangerous, dear. There's safety in numbers and as a nurse, you know well enough how to deal with men when they get a bit too fruity. But on the plus side, you can get about £100 a time and you wouldn't be out of the flat for more than an hour or two at a time."

"No, I'll have to think of something else." And the matter was left there.

But Briony thought about the idea for a few days and under severe financial pressure, came to the conclusion that she could bring herself to give it a try if it meant keeping the car. So when she bumped into Beryl again, she asked, "I've been thinking about our conversation the other day. How would I go about trying a strippagram thing?"

"You go to an agency. They advertise and then send you a job when something suitable comes in."

"Do you get any training?"

"I don't think so. You train on the job. They say the first is the worst and after that it becomes easier." So Briony decided to give it a try. Just the once to see if she could manage it.

# Chapter Nine

Spooner and Lanes, as they eventually decided to call themselves, were going from strength to strength with a steady flow of work from the council and from other sources, so much so that it was necessary for them to find bigger premises to accommodate the extra workforce and store all the equipment. Vic had been looking at possibilities and decided to rent a complex comprising a secure yard with a number of outbuildings plus a decent suite of offices. It was a little more than the firm needed at the moment but Vic had ideas about letting off part until they grew into it. He had been introduced to a central heating engineer called Maurice Horton and he had carried out some very keenly priced sub contracts so when Horton said he was looking for premises, Vic offered him a lock up big enough to accommodate his white van with a plastic tube on the roof rack and yet leave room to move about and do a few jobs.

For some reason which he couldn't explain, Ben didn't quite trust Horton. He was a good worker but at the prices he charged, seemed to have a sight more money that was reasonable and he was flashing it about too often. Ben could only put it down to an easy-come-easy-go attitude and constantly wondered about his integrity. And as for that big

Mercedes he ran – that was just too much. It wasn't just that either. Horton had some strange comings and goings late at night which Ben vaguely observed when he was working late. There were times when things were being loaded from Horton's to another vehicle and cash changing hands but it wasn't Ben's business so he let it pass.

Ben mentioned his misgivings to Vic who would hear nothing against the man. "So long as he pays his rent and keeps on putting in keen prices, I don't care what he does in his spare time."

Ben wasn't so sure.

It was while Ben was in town one day to do a bit of personal shopping that he heard a familiar voice from behind. "Well! If it isn't my old cellmate, Ben. How are you doing? Still knocking old men down for their money, I hope."

Ben was mortified. This was the voice of Jacko whom Ben had met inside and the last thing he wanted now was to be seen in public with this man, never mind have the conversation overheard. But Jacko wasn't one to be shrugged off easily. He had been the prisoner who knew all the ropes, how to get favours from the screws, how to get the best jobs and how to get other prisoners into or out of trouble according to how well he liked you. If it hadn't been for his comparative youth, he would have been an old lag.

Ben felt the friendly arm flung across his shoulder.

"Jacko. Fancy meeting you," said Ben as quietly as he could, really hoping to quieten the other man as well. "How long have you been out?"

Jacko put on a mock stern face. "Never ask an old cellmate that, Ben, it gives the wrong impression." Ben was in a quandary. He didn't want to carry on this conversation but he couldn't bring it to a sudden stop without drawing attention to it. He decided to feign friendship as the best means of getting away quickly.

"What are you doing with yourself now?" It was a question Ben couldn't avoid answering.

"Actually I've gone back into the building game," Ben offered lamely.

"Well then, as it happens, I might just be able to help you there, young Ben."

"I don't really need any help right now."

"Rubbish, we all need a bit of help. Now in the building game you're going to need materials, my lad, and I happen to be able to get the stuff at, shall we say, knock down prices."

"Jacko, you're just asking to be sent back inside."

"Not me, Ben, I'm too smart for that. All I am is a telephone number. You tell me what you want, I have it delivered wherever you say and then I collect the money. I don't actually touch the stuff myself. It's a dream. I can't go wrong."

Ben was now trying to get out of a fix. "Look, Jacko, it's kind of you to think of me but I'm only in a small way of business. I wouldn't have any orders big enough to interest you."

"No matter, old son. I've got a man down this area who regularly buys from me. All you need to do is put your small order though to him and he'll deliver when he gets his own consignment. I'll give you his name." Jacko wrote on a piece of paper and handed it to Ben then said, "Sorry, I couldn't invite you for a drink but I'm on a tight schedule. Nice to have seen you." And with that he disappeared into a limo with the windows so dark that Ben doubted whether he could see out of them, never mind in.

Ben was glad to see the back of him, no mistake, he'd keep a sharper lookout in future.

It wasn't until he got home that Ben looked at the piece of-paper. It had Maurice Horton's name and telephone number on it. This was confirmation of everything that Ben had feared and he felt obliged to go to Vic again with this new evidence.

He called round to Vic's house on the following morning, Sunday. Mrs Spooner met him at the door. "Hello, Ben. Have you got Penny with you?"

"No. I thought she might be here. Perhaps she's gone shopping or something."

"That means you've come on business I suppose. Go on through – Vic's out the back so I'll get a couple of beers for you."

They sat in the garden together, the three of them and Ben explained how he had met Jacko and what had transpired. "I think Horton will have to go, Vic," Ben concluded. "We can't have him using the yard for criminal activities or we'll all be in it together and with my record, I'm very sensitive to this sort of thing."

"I don't think I ought to condemn the man on the say-so of a known criminal," Vic responded. "You might find yourself in a similar position one day and you wouldn't like to be condemned like that."

Ben thought that Vic was stretching his good nature too far and Mrs Spooner must have seen it in his face so, ever the one with a compromise, she suggested. "Look, Vic. Why don't you make a few surreptitious enquiries at Rotary Lunch tomorrow. Someone else is bound to know something about him but be careful. I know what you are for blabbing your mouth and you don't want to give Horton a chance to sue you for slander."

"Me!" protested Vic. "I can be as surreptitious as the next man. But it's a good idea and I'll do it."

When Vic arrived for lunch, there were not too many present but Carruthers was at the bar with his usual gin and tonic. "Hello, John. I'm glad I met you. Wanted to have a quiet word about something." Carruthers seemed surprised at such an approach from Spooner.

"What's up? Having trouble with that jailbird clerk of works."

"No, nothing of the sort and he's a damn fine chap as it happens. No, it's my tenant in the yard, a chap by the name of Horton, Maurice Horton. Just wondered if you knew anything about him that's all."

"Wouldn't touch him with a bargepole. The man's a crook," replied Carruthers with all discretion he could muster. "Here comes Jones. Ask him."

Jones the solicitor came up to the bar and expressed surprise to find Spooner and Carruthers apparently in polite conversation together. "What's going on?" he enquired.

Carruthers took over, rather too loudly for Vic's liking, "He wants to know whether it's safe to trust Maurice Horton, that's all."

"That crook!" replied Jones. "If I were to shake hands with him, I'd count my fingers afterwards. Why do you want to know?"

"Well, as a matter of fact," said Vic, "I just wanted to know whether he is reliable." But by now Vic was as convinced as he needed to be.

Vic called a family conference. "What Ben said is all true," he began. "I'm sorry I doubted your word, lad, but there's no denying that he's no good and first thing tomorrow, I'm going to tell him to go, no ifs or buts. But before I do that, I want to check on how we stand on outstanding jobs because he'll be thrown off them as well."

"You can't just throw him out and leave him to carry on with his crooked ways," piped up Penny. "He'll just go on doing the same thing somewhere else."

"What else can we do?" it was Ben now. "After all we haven't got any real evidence and if you take that to the police, they'll do nothing."

"Well, that's not good enough for me," she came back. "At least I'm going to try to find out where he's been getting the stuff from so that we can warn the wholesalers."

"How?" a chorus from the other three.

"There can't be that many firms big enough to supply in the quantities we're talking about. At least I can phone round and try."

Nobody wanted to argue with Penny when she was in this frame of mind and in any case, they all thought that her enquiries would get nowhere so it was left that Penny could have just 24 hours to come up with something.

As it happened, it turned out to be very easy. Penny had a charming telephone manner and rarely had difficulty in getting through to a managing director. On only the fourth call, she discovered a firm that had been systematically losing stock and it didn't take long to compare dates and quantities before it became clear that there was stolen stock on two or possibly three of Vic's contracts. When he found that out, he was furious. So he didn't confront Horton with the information as he intended, instead, he gave Penny a bit more time.

Stovepipes Inc. was a big set up near Coventry and once Penny had her father's consent, she telephoned to make an arrangement to travel down on the next day to lay her plans. As an afterthought, she added, "It might be a good idea to have somebody from your insurance company there as well."

She told Ben that evening that she would be off to Coventry in the morning. "What on earth for?" he asked.

"I'm going to set up a sting," was her mysterious reply.

It was a highly successful meeting and on her return, she called a family conference to explain what she had arranged.

"It's very clear," she began, "that the plumbing stuff is being stolen to order and we can tell that by comparing what we have required for certain jobs with what has been stolen a matter of days beforehand, so all we have to do is to trick Horton into an argument with this Jacko chap so that things come out into the open. What I've arranged is that Stovepipes Inc. will provide us with 5 condensing boilers and 40 radiators with all the valves, pump and everything that's going to be needed for the Grange Road flat conversion. The thing is that it will all be cleaned up second hand gear, not new."

"How will that help?" queried Vic.

"Hold on and I'll tell you," she replied. "We know from past experience that Horton always has his van locked up in the shed before he starts a job, and he keeps the van double locked as well because he's got all the gear in there ready. Now, we get his keys then when he is away, we swap the stolen stuff for the second-hand stuff. When Horton finds out, he'll go rushing off to Jacko and we'll have him followed. Then, with luck, Jacko will go off for a row with the actual thieves and we'll have the whole gang. Just for good measure, Stovepipes Inc. are going to install a secret video camera because they are convinced that the thieves are getting help from one of their security people and they want him caught as well."

"Now hold on a minute," said Vic. "Have you thought about how we might do all this. You can't just walk up to a man and borrow his keys without him smelling a rat, can you?"

"It's all worked out, daddy, don't worry. Mr Cutler the key cutter has given me these little plasticine trays. All we need is to have the keys for a few seconds to make impressions and Mr Cutler reckons he can produce a set within the hour. So, when Horton comes in, as he always does, a week before the start to collect the sub-contract, I'll distract him by wearing something that shows off my best bits – he always ogles me anyway; then daddy can take the keys from where he always leaves them beside his mobile. Ben can be in the back office waiting to make the impressions and you can put the keys back without him knowing that they've been gone."

"Well, I don't know," said Vic. "It all sounds a bit dodgy to me."

"Oh, come on, daddy, nothing will go wrong, you'll see."

Mrs Spooner sat quietly saying nothing. Deep down she knew that the scheme was full of unknowns that could cause it to go wrong but she also knew that Penny was both resourceful and lucky. She decided to go along with it thus far anyway and if they did get the keys, she might take a bit of control. They all agreed to give it a shot.

The appointment for Horton to come in to collect the contract was made for 10 am on the Friday just over a week before start date. All four were in the office at their stations before 9 am and Penny was wearing a very low-cut dress which they all found at once disturbing and reassuring. By 10 am, there was no sign of Horton and Mrs Spooner could see that the others were getting very jumpy. This would not do so she decided to calm them all down with coffee. The kettle had boiled so it was a matter of seconds to pour out three polystyrene beakers of hot coffee which she took round to each of them. No sooner had she done so than in came Horton as expected, straight up to Vic's desk where he plonked his mobile and his car keys, all as anticipated.

Vic and Horton exchanged the usual pleasant greetings and then Vic started to shuffle through the papers on his desk as if he was looking for Horton's contract. Penny took her cue and stood up, walked over to the filing cabinet, pulled out the very bottom drawer and leaned over it looking for something. To say that she was causing a diversion was an understatement. Ben was looking indignantly, Vic was looking in wonder but Horton was leeching, no doubt about that. But it wasn't working quite well enough because no matter how Horton ogled Penny's best bits he didn't move his hand far enough from the keys to give Vic a chance to snaffle them. Penny could see her plan going wrong so she decided to add a bit of spice. Suddenly she stood up with a little squeal, said something about the rough edges on the furniture and pulled her skirt up to her waist to complain that she had ruined another pair of tights. This clinched it but not the way Penny thought. Horton was fairly drooling at the sight and moved his hand away so Vic made his move, but he too was watching Penny instead of the keys with the result that his hand hit the polystyrene beaker and shot nearly half a pint of scalding coffee all over Horton's best bits. He gave a yell and jumped up, ran to the toilet where he mopped himself up and by the time he came back with a large brown stain on his jeans right where he would have preferred not to have such a stain, the impressions were half way to Mr Cutler and the keys back where he had left them.

Vic could barely contain his mirth as he handed over the contract. Penny now had her head bent over the typewriter apparently having a coughing fit and Mrs Spooner was hiding behind the door of the back office. As soon as Horton was out of earshot, they all collapsed into helpless laughter.

They were in a state of high excitement at having succeeded and beginning to think what a clever lot they were when Mrs Spooner poured cold water over their euphoria.

"Today," she pronounced, "we were very lucky indeed. If the rest of this plan is to succeed, we must plan much more carefully so I'll be taking control."

There was no arguing with Mrs Spooner when she was in this mood. "Family conference after dinner tonight. Right!"

The family conference was a serious one. They all identified the following Friday as the best time to swap the gear in Horton's van for the second-hand stuff currently hidden in their own workshop. It wasn't until Mrs Spooner pointed out that it would take two people about two hours to do the swap that they began to wonder how they could be certain not to be interrupted. After all, they all knew that

Horton kept strange hours and might roll up any time. Ben came up with a solution.

"Always, before the start of a job, Vic takes Horton to the pub where they programme the job and arrange attendance by other tradesmen so that's the obvious time for us three to do the swap. It will be up to you, Vic, to make sure that you keep him there for two hours."

"Too dangerous," cut in Mrs Spooner. "I suggest that you put a wheel clamp on Horton's car in the pub car park and I'll drop Vic off so that neither of them have transport. I can't see Horton coming back here in a taxi leaving his Mere in a pub car park. Vic, you will have to bear the brunt of Horton's wrath as best you can but you should have no difficulty in holding him there for two hours if his car is stuck." They all thought the plan fool-proof and well worth the trouble to see this gang caught.

"For safety," Mrs Spooner continued, "I will position myself across the road from the pub once you two are safely inside and we will all have mobile telephones switched on. For the sake of not wasting time, we shall all be numbered. I am No 1, Vic, you are No 2, Penny No 3, you Ben will be No 4 and last but not least, Horton will be No 5. Now have you all got that?"

Yes, they all had that and chose not to argue with it. Mrs Spooner had spoken with an authority that she rarely showed.

That week passed slowly. Once the plan was agreed, they all wanted to get on with it and so did Mrs Spooner because she knew very well that the more they thought about it, the more problems they might imagine. But when Friday evening arrived, they were all still resolute so they set about the job. It was Ben who took Vic to the pub. He dropped him off in the car park at ten past seven and was surprised that Horton's car wasn't there. "That's not like him," remarked Vic, "he keeps good time as a rule." Ben told him not to worry, he'd wait out of sight until the Mere showed up and then clamp it.

So when Vic got inside and found Horton already propping up the bar with a drink, he was surprised. It was usually quiet in the saloon bar at this time of the evening but there was obviously a party going on in the back room because Vic could hear rugby songs being sung rather loudly. Mavis pulled him a pint because the landlord was serving a great Neanderthal of a chap with a tray full of pints of lager and was busy trying to find enough glasses.

"Evening, Maurice," he greeted Horton. "Not driving tonight?"

"Yes, what makes you ask?"

"Nothing really, I just didn't see your car in the car park that's all."

"Oh, it's in for a service. I've come in my wife's car. You probably noticed that horrible little purple Peugeot out there."

Vic hadn't but he said he had.

They started the meeting and after a few minutes Vic excused himself and went to the toilet. He called up Ben. "Hello 4, this is 2. 5 is in a purple Peugeot."

"What's the number plate?"

"Don't be daft, man. If I ask him that, he'll smell a rat for sure. How many purple Peugeots do you think you might find?"

"Sorry 2. I'll pop down now and fix it."

Vic washed his hands and went back into the bar.

Briony Freshwater was on her first assignment and very nervous. She had been over and over it in her mind and finally the time had come for her to do her party piece. She had been rigged out in a costume that looked like rugby shirt and shorts but it was only held together with bits of Velcro and wasn't that comfortable. She drove up to the front of the pub and parked her purple Peugeot right in front of the door on the forecourt, spurning the car park in case she wanted to get away quickly. As she stepped inside, she almost cannoned into Vic coming back from the toilet. Vic looked at her and smiled which gave her a bit of confidence to ask him, "Do you know a Horace Moreton?"

Vic, pointed to Maurice Horton and said, "That's him."

Briony walked over to Horton feeling that it was now or never. She opened her purse, took out a little piece of paper and recited.

"We've won the cup, we've scored the tries. Your captaincy's been very wise.

"We're glad to give you our support an' happy birthday, Horace Moreton."

And with a flourish, she reached around and grabbed the Velcro edge whipped off her costume which she cast to the floor and stood there in front of Horton wearing only her high heels and a thong thing. The effect was electrifying. Vic's eyes nearly popped out of his head. Horton soon realised the mistake but decided to make the most of it and the Neanderthal at the bar also realised the mistake and came striding over. He grabbed Briony's arm and tried to drag her away, saying, "You've got the wrong party – over here."

Whatever Horton was, he didn't care to see a lady mistreated. He stood up and confronted the rugby player. "Leave her alone you great lout – don't you know how to treat a lady."

"Who are you calling a lout?" and he swung a punch at Horton's head which would have flattened him if it had connected. But Horton was still sober, unlike his assailant, so he was easily able to sidestep the punch, as a result of which Vic took it on the top of his head, completely knocking him off balance. As Vic fell, he crashed his head on the edge of the table and fell unconscious right on top of Briony's discarded costume. While the rugby player was off balance, Horton caught him with a haymaker right on the button which had him staggering back the way he had come and as the landlord rose from behind the counter triumphantly holding two more glasses that he had found, a flailing arm sent the thirteen full ones flying all over him. They had had trouble in this pub before. Quick as you like, the barmaid was on the phone to the police and the landlord stepped through from behind the counter with a truncheon in his hand. Then the dividing door flew open and in came fifteen drunken rugby players demanding to know where their drinks were.

What they saw took their minds off the lager completely. Vic had recovered consciousness to find a naked young lady with her arms around his neck frantically trying to retrieve her costume. Vic decided that he liked this so he feigned blankness so that she continued. The rugby team had gathered round and were urging Briony to do whatever it was they thought she was doing to Vic and the Neanderthal had picked himself up and started on Horton again. Poor Briony was petrified. She abandoned her costume, grabbed her purse and ran out to her car which she started up only to find the engine stall when she tried to move off. She sat there and beat her hands in frustration on the steering wheel not knowing what to do next when the doors flew open and the pub fight spilled out onto the forecourt. Not too soon, the police arrived and in a matter of minutes, six well organised men had the whole shebang shut up in a black Maria, including Horton.

From her observation point across the road, Mrs Spooner watched all this in amazement. She dialled Penny on her mobile. "Hello 3, this is 1. 2 has cocked up. 4 has clamped the wrong car, 5 has been arrested," and in a trailing off voice added, "and I do believe that your father is staggering out of the pub with that naked girl's clothes over his arm."

Penny said, "Hello 1, this is 3. Would you repeat that last bit about my father?" But Mrs Spooner was out of the car and across the road where she quickly positioned herself between Vic and Briony. "I'll take that," she said snatching the costume from Vic as she slipped into the passenger seat and used her own body to shield the poor girl from prying eyes.

She helped the girl into her skimpy clothes and when she was decent and calmed down a bit she asked, "Was this your first time?"

"Yes, actually it was. How did you know?"

"Never mind that," she replied. "Those agencies don't change. They really ought to warn you to take a spare frock. Sometimes these things get torn to bits in the excitement." They chatted on until Ben came and removed the clamp then waved her a cheery goodbye.

After she had driven off, Vic turned to his wife with a huge question in his eyes.

"Don't even ask," she said before Vic could speak. "Just keep on telling people that I used to be in show business – but you don't have to tell them what I showed."

At 8 am sharp next morning, Vic was at the police station to bail Horton out. By 9.30, Horton was on site and by midday, Ben arrived to point out to Horton what he had already discovered – the gear was all substandard or second hand. Horton's face was purple with rage. He was on his mobile calling somebody a thieving twister or something less polite and then in his van driving off to meet somebody. The rest was easy. Two insurance investigators followed him to Jacko and took long-distance photographs of the altercation. Then they trailed Jacko to a dingy basement on the north side of the town where they photographed two scruffy individuals who also showed up on the secret video camera at Stovepipes Inc. along with a nice picture of the bent security man. The police were able to bag the whole gang.

# Chapter Ten

After the excitement of trapping robbers, Vic felt a little deflated as did the rest of his family. He was too busy to get to Rotary lunch on the Monday after the operation so it was a week later that he came into the bar to be almost feted by his fellow Rotarians who had read of the coup by then in the local paper. They slapped him on the back, shook his hand and asked him how he proposed to celebrate his success but Vic hadn't really thought about that. After lunch, the president stood up and made a speech about the bravery and endeavour of Vic and his family in tackling this gang, all of which seemed a bit over the top to Vic because to him and the others it had been more of lark than a serious undertaking. But the club wanted to applaud him so who was he to say otherwise. So after the president's speech, Vic got to his feet to reply.

"What we did was no more than our civic duty," he began with all humility, "and whilst I appreciate the good wishes of my fellow Rotarians, I am sure that any of you would have done the same if the opportunity were to present itself. But I'll assure you that we shall be doing a little celebrating as a family because I propose to take them all out on Saturday night for a maledictory veal at the Majestic." His mistake was greeted with a little laughter and a lot of good wishes except from Carruthers who sat there po-faced throughout as though he were not joining in. It so happened that Carruthers had a nephew who was secretary of the rugby club and the version that he had been told had Spooner and Horton gate crashing someone else's party and Vic grabbing the strippagram girl and trying to rape her. So it wasn't surprising that Carruthers felt sour that Vic was getting all this adulation. It was perfectly clear however that to bring that up here would only result in being shouted down and cast as a bad loser. But he wasn't going to let Vic get away with it. He decided that it was about time he took Mrs Carruthers out to dinner – and Saturday at the Majestic would do very nicely.

When Saturday arrived, Vic and his family got dressed up and ordered a mini bus to transport them. They all noticed a strange look on the head waiter's face as they walked in. To be fair, the Majestic had not blackballed the Spooners but it was evident that they had not been forgotten. they were shown to a table just a little out of the way, that's all.

The meal was, as ever, quite delicious and after the main course, Vic summoned the waiter and asked to see the sweet menu. "We don't actually have a sweet menu now, Sir. We have all the sweets on a trolley."

"That's new," said Vic with a question in his voice.

"A management decision, Sir, it reduces the amount of traffic in and out of the kitchen. You may remember, Sir, on your last visit, there was a bit of an incident?"

"How could I forget," replied Vic wondering what was coming next.

"I'll ask Alphonse to bring the trolley over in a minute or two, Sir."

"Thanks," said a relieved Vic. "And could you ask the wine waiter to bring some champagne as well?"

"Certainly, Sir."

When the champagne arrived, Vic asked the wine waiter to leave it so that they could drink a toast after they had eaten their sweet.

"I shall have to open it for you," he said.

"That's OK," said Vic. "I'll do it."

"No, Sir, I'll do it. A management decision, Sir, you may remember when you were last here?"

"Yes, I do," said Vic now beginning to think that the place had changed a lot on his account which made him feel a little guilty.

The waiter poured them a glass each and left the rest in a bucket on the end of the table. Vic stood up and raised a glass, then said to the others, "I think we should drink a toast to the success of our first attempt at crime stopping."

"Just a minute," said Penny.

Mrs Spooner said, "Don't start that again, I'm going to drink mine while it's still bubbly so good health." The others did the same.

As Vic stood up to take the bottle and pour another glass, who should come in but Mr and Mrs Carruthers. Vic was actually pleased to see them and waved them over.

"Come and have a drink with us," he invited.

"What for?" said Carruthers, "To celebrate your part in wrestling a naked girl to the floor at somebody else's party. I think not, old man."

Vic's hackles rose. "Now look here, John, you've got it all wrong."

"That's not what I hear. I suppose your family are proud of the way you behaved?"

Mrs Carruthers was far from pleased. "John, what are you doing? I thought you had brought me here for dinner, not for an argument. Come away."

But Carruthers hadn't finished yet. "I happen to know the secretary of the rugby club so I know what really went on in there."

Ben intervened, "What went on in that pub was just a misunderstanding, that's all."

Mrs Carruthers was now pulling her husband's arm but he wouldn't budge. He addressed Ben contemptuously, "When I want the opinion of a jailbird, I'll ask for it."

Mrs Spooner who had sat through all this silently gave the ice bucket a seemingly accidental shove and as it lay down on the table top the contents poured all over Carruthers' trousers and Mrs Carruthers' feet. The lady stepped back sharply away from the deluge as the icy water caught her, just as Alphonse was pulling the sweet trolley behind her causing her to sit upon something soft and squidgy.

The sweet trolley saved her from falling over but she was clearly furious. "John Carruthers," she fairly bellowed. "Can't you just take me out to dinner without having to cause a scene." And she turned and walked out with her husband in pursuit of her elegantly, white satin clad bottom with two large patches of chocolate and two strategically positioned red cherries.

The Spooner family did not laugh. They all choked it back admirably until Alphonse announce, "Black Forest Gateaux's off." Then they laughed and laughed so much that the head waiter and the wine waiter both came over to see what they could do.

This time they decided that there would have to be a black mark against the name Spooner for the sake of the restaurant's good name and the sanity of the staff.

When they finally got home, Mrs Spooner remembered that she had interrupted Penny just as her husband had been proposing a toast. "What were you going to say when you tried to delay things, Penny. You know, just when your father was about to make a toast?"

"Oh, nothing much. It's just that I heard from the insurance company today that on conviction of that gang of thieves, we will be entitled to a reward."

"How much?" the other three enquired in unison.

"Well, I expect it to be what I asked for when I went up to Coventry," she replied, teasing them by delaying.

"Yes, but how much?"

"A matter of £5000 if you must know."

It was a matter of months before the reward money came along and during that time, they had all had time to think about what should be done with it. It arrived in the form of a cheque payable to Penny so she called a family conference.

"I think we should either divide it into four or else decide together what to do with it. What do you think?"

The reluctance to speak first was obvious but it was Ben who had the courage to start the ball rolling. "I've given this a lot of thought over the last few weeks and I can't help feeling a bit guilty about taking a reward for simply doing what we had to do. The way I see it is that, if rewards are paid, it will only encourage people to behave properly for money and that must be wrong. I don't mean to get at you, Penny, for arranging it but I'd rather not accept it."

That was a long speech for Ben who tended to keep his counsel and go along with the others but that made his viewpoint all the more compelling. They were all quiet for a long time until Mrs Spooner decided that what Ben had said was really quite right so she said so.


"Well, we can't very well give it back," said Vic. "That would be worse because it would just be absorbed into the profits of the insurance company and they make enough already."

"I'm not saying we should give it back," said Ben. "What we ought to do is find a worthwhile cause to donate it to."

They were all quiet for a while longer, then Mrs Spooner brightened up. "I know the very thing," she declared. "It's easy to forget where all this started and poor Elsie Mann who lost all her savings just because she tried to help Mrs Lee. She's the one who has come out badly all through this as we have gathered from talk at the WI."

"Are you suggesting," said Vic, "that we should give it to Elsie? I don't know the lady myself but from what I've heard, she'd be unlikely to accept a gift from us. The very idea of taking charity from a firm of builders would upset her, I'm sure."

"Yes, but do you agree to the principle?"

"Actually, yes I do," said Vic with uncommon sincerity. Penny nodded her assent as well.

Ben said, "That will suit me very well indeed and if I might make a suggestion, we could make the gift anonymous so that she would be in no position to refuse it."

"How do you mean? If you send it through the post, she'll see who wrote the cheque and you can't very well bung five grand through her letter box without scaring the lady."

Penny interjected, "Why not ask the Reverend Thornthwaite to give it to her on our behalf. He would be totally discreet and we would know that she had received it without worrying about it."

"That's a good idea," said Mrs Spooner. "Vic, you can have a quiet word with him at Rotary on Monday. I'm sure he'll agree."

And so it was arranged.

When Vic arrived at Rotary on Monday, Reverend Thornthwaite was in a very jolly frame of mind and, quite out of character, offered to buy Vic a drink.

"Very kind of you, old man. I'll just have an orange juice if you please. As a matter of fact, I wanted to ask a favour if you can spare the time."

"Well, if it's going to take time, it all depends on how much but fire away."

"You know, just as everyone else here seems to know, that there was a substantial reward for nabbing that gang a few months back."

"And well-earned if I may say so," Theodore responded.

"You may say so if you wish but you haven't reckoned with my family. They all think it immoral to take a reward for doing what we all ought to do if the occasion arises, that is to say our civic duty." Theodore was chastened by this because it was the sort of thing he should be saying rather than receiving.

"Well, of course you are quite right but so few people see it that way nowadays."

"Well, my lot do, so they have decided that the reward money should go to Elsie Mann to replace what she lost when old Mrs Lee died suddenly."

"What a capital idea." Theodore was beaming. He remembered telling Elsie at the time that the Lord would provide and somehow he felt vindicated by this offer. He checked himself for thinking such a thought.

"The thing is," Vic went on, "is how we are going to get it to her. She'll never accept charity form us so if the gift is anonymous, she can't very well refuse." Vic wondered why Theodore's face had started to show concern. Quite simply it was because he was beginning to realise that he was going to be asked to go to Elsie and give her the money. He faced up to it.

"I suppose you would like me to do the deed on your behalf?" he queried.

"Exactly," said Vic. "You of all people can be tactful and keep the Spooner name out of it. That would please us very much."

He agreed to do it but failed to enjoy his lunch because the prospect of going to see Elsie bore down on him. For sure she would misunderstand and for all he knew, she might make a pass at him in excitement or something. Oh dear, this was going to be so difficult. Why hadn't he joined the army as his father had wanted. But this wouldn't do. If the Spooners could do their duty then he, Theodore Thornthwaite, would not shrink from doing his. That afternoon he phoned Elsie and arranged to see her. He wasn't prepared to discuss the reason on the telephone which made the prospect for Elsie all the more exciting. She would make tea and buy some special cake.

Theodore arrived at Elsie's house on the following afternoon in a business-like frame of mind. Elsie looked a little flushed with excitement when she answered the door, the kettle was on and tea made before Theodore could get down to the business he had called about so he contented himself with the exchange of small talk until his mouth was not occupied by other things. Then he began.

"I've called today, Elsie, for a very particular reason. You may not know it but in this town, there are some fine people of high principle who have come upon good fortune, good fortune I might add, that they do not feel they deserve. Now it so happens that these good souls wish to direct their good fortune to a more deserving cause which is why I am here."

By this time, Elsie's expression had begun to change from excited anticipation to something more resembling bewilderment. He went on. "Remembering that you yourself were good enough to consider old Mrs Lee and the consequence of doing so, these fine people have asked me to pass onto you the benefit of their good fortune by recompensing you for the money you lost when the old lady died." Elsie's face was changed again, now bearing a look of near horror as the meaning of the visit began to sink in. "So I am very glad indeed to have been entrusted to give you this £5000 anonymously on their behalf." As he handed over the package of money, Elsie had a look of utter mortification. She realised that if it had really been Theodore who left that money in the church for her all that time ago, he would not be on this mission now. Which meant that she had been harbouring feelings for him based on a false understanding and that, in all probability, he didn't reciprocate those feeling at all. He must have wondered why she looked at him as she did. She would never recover from the shame of this, could not possibly face him again. Then she realised the other consequence of her misunderstanding. She had stolen money from the church and that was sacrilege.

She turned away from Theodore, tears filling her eyes, then ran from the room leaving the reverend gentleman sitting helplessly by the tea things without the least idea why she was so upset. But he had done what he had come to do and he had no idea what he could do to console Elsie even if he had known where she had gone so after what seemed a lot longer than a few minutes, he called, "I'll let myself out," and departed.

On the way back to the vicarage, he wondered what on earth it was all about and what one could possibly do to understand a woman's mind.

Elsie sat alone and sad at home. She went over the events of the meeting and couldn't possibly come to any other conclusion than the one she had already arrived at. She looked at the brown paper package of money, so reminiscent of the other brown paper package she had taken from the church. It even had the same rubber stamp across the flap. She went sadly to her box of treasures and took out the empty package that she had kept as a memento of what she had thought was Theodore's secret love for her and she knew then what she had to do. She took the money from the package and rewrapped it in the original package still marked with the words, "An anonymous donation." Then she wrote a letter to the Rev Thornthwaite saying that she could no longer clean the church brass and hoping that he would soon find a replacement. Then sadly she took her bicycle to the church, let herself in by the vestry door and carefully placed the package behind the cross on the altar from whence she had taken it. Next she placed her letter where Theodore would find it when he came to write the sermon, let herself out and locked the door behind her. Finally, she posted her key of the vestry back through the letter box.

# Chapter Eleven

Ben was to be introduced to Rotary Club so he was dressed very smartly on the Monday morning when he got to the office. He really wasn't that interested but was allowing himself to be taken along just to please Vic. They set off soon after midday so that Ben could be introduced to as many members as possible before lunch began. Theodore was there earlier than usual and looking perplexed. Vic greeted him and made the introduction then set about getting a drink in.

"You seem a bit preoccupied this morning," he ventured, trying to get a conversation started for the sake of Ben who otherwise would stand and say nothing.

"Actually I'm very puzzled," replied Theo.

"Did you manage to give that you know what to you know who?" Vic asked as mysteriously as possible.

"Oh! That. Yes, that was OK. Although I can't for the life of me understand why you know who acted so strangely about it. No, I'm puzzled about something quite different. I went to the church on Saturday morning and found an anonymous donation behind the altar cross. I think you must have started a season of goodwill all on your own. It just happened to be £5000 and I wondered whether you had anything to do with it that's all." He produced the brown package with the writing on it. Ben saw it and recognised it immediately.

"The thing is," went on Theodore, "that anybody might have picked this up. I know we keep the church locked up most of the time but not always under close security. This seems to have been a very insecure hiding place to me."

Ben checked himself from saying that it must be about the best hiding place in the world because he had personally placed it behind the altar about three years ago.

But none of them could begin to explain why it had happened. Only Elsie Mann knew that. Theodore said, "I could have done with that when the roof was leaking."

# Chapter Twelve

Wendy Blowers and Joyce Green were inseparable enemies at school forever arguing about clothes, boyfriends, personal belongings and appearance but they never ever argued about who was the most academically inclined because both had decided at an early age that high achievement at school was not for them. It wasn't that they were lazy or stupid but each had recognised that success would have to be by guile, graft or selection of a suitable husband. In the latter ambition, however, they were as different as chalk and cheese because Wendy knew that she could settle for modest security in a happy relationship whereas Joyce hankered after power and authority. As they grew older, the bickering diminished because they contrived to keep apart and when finally they left school and went their separate ways, they hardly expected to meet again.

Wendy was very much a child of the fifties. She had a good singing voice and could perform all the latest songs almost as well as the original performers. Some of her contemporaries urged her to take up singing as a career, not easily done without a bit of money to get started and support from home which was definitely not forthcoming. She took a job in a factory which she utterly detested but was careful enough to save some of her wages so that she could buy some suitable fancy clothes for performing and to get some professionally taken photographs to take around to the agencies in the hope of getting some singing work. But it took a lot of foot slogging and a long time before anything worthwhile came along and even then, it wasn't all that good. But it was an improvement on working in a factory.

Joyce trod an entirely different path. Her parents paid for her to go to secretarial college where she did rather better than she had done at school and also gave her the opportunity to refine her manners thus enabling her to find work which called for charm and personality rather than skill. As a personal assistant, she did very well and moved in the circles where she could meet more suitable young men. When she met Harold Dixon-Rhudders, she decided right away that he would become her husband one day in spite of the fact that he was smaller than Joyce by a good few inches and was a touch portly for one so young. On the plus side, he was close to the end of a military career which would provide a good pension and was also the son of an MP. There was money in this family and no mistake.

It took a while for Joyce to get her man but she succeeded in spite of attempts by other more suitable ladies to win him. But by flattery and pseudo subservience, he came to believe that Joyce would make less impossible demands upon him than most women which would enable him to lead the life that he preferred. When Harold's father died, Joyce was there urging him on to take over as the local MP which, in the event, proved to be only a matter of declaring that he was available because the name was known, there were no black marks against it, and the selection committee had nobody else to turn to. So Harold was elected and continued in the sedentary steps of his father, going to any length of silence so as to avoid making waves. Joyce was left very much to her own devices because Harold moved up to London for most of the time occasionally deigning to come down to the constituency. So she took up politics at a local level and was soon doing her bit on the town council, an occupation which she enjoyed immensely and which pleased Harold no end because he was able to boast about it at Westminster.

Wendy had not been quite so lucky in the marriage stakes and was still unattached by the age of 27. To say that her singing career had taken off would be an overstatement of some magnitude but she had, nevertheless, become a professional singer. An agency had fixed her up with a series of local gigs in clubs and even special occasions in pubs or hotels but it was very hard work, not at all glamorous and didn't even pay quite enough to make ends meet so she had to resort to all sorts of escort and other work sometimes. It was on a Saturday evening that her life changed. Friday had been busy with two gigs on opposite sides of the town and on the Saturday, she was similarly booked. What she had to do was arrive early at the first venue then do her 20-minute slot. The Radical club had a good dance floor upstairs and the members were all keen ballroom dancers but the band had to have a refreshment break so Wendy was booked to keep the place lively while the band was off. Her act was sung to pre-recorded tapes while the members mostly went back and forth replenishing their drinks and so on. She certainly didn't consider herself to be the main attraction. When she finished, she had to put on an old pair of trousers and a hooded fleece over the tights and sequins, then cycle across town to do the same thing in a slightly more glamorous club.

As she was wheeling her bike out of the secretary's office, she was approached by a young man, perhaps a couple of years older than herself, whom she had often noticed as being one of the few members to pay any attention to her act.

"Can I buy you a drink?" he asked.

"I'd love to accept but right now I have to get my skates on and get across to the Astoria for another gig."

"Perhaps I should make you a better offer," he persisted.

"Like what?" Wendy continued the conversation knowing that she really ought not to but she definitely liked this young man and really wanted him to keep talking.

"Like, marry me and let me take you away from all this. Will that do?" It was said in jest but with just a hint of something more serious. Enough anyway to make Wendy decide to abandon her second gig so as to see what might develop.

"That's a bit strong for starters. Try something else."

"OK. Let's eat."

"You're on," she said, "but where. I'm hungry that's for sure but I happen to be dressed like a tart underneath and a tramp on top so it's going to be hard to choose a suitable place even if I agree."

"You say yes, that's all. I know the very place."

"Very well. Yes then."

Wendy had no idea why she had acted on impulse to the possible detriment of her admittedly shaky career but she had a feeling that this was the man for her. Later, as they sat with bacon sandwiches and steaming mugs of tea on a traffic island between the iron railings and white tiled stairways leading to the underground lavatories, she knew that she had made a good choice.

He said, "My name's Spooner, Vic Spooner. I'm in the building game. What's yours?"

All that had been years ago and was, indirectly, the means of bringing back into contact the two inseparable enemies of their schooldays. Joyce's political career had moved on and she was now the mayor elect. On the evening of her inauguration, the council had arranged a reception at the ratepayers' expense to welcome the new mayor and introduce her to certain influential people of the town. The president of Rotary for the current year was Jones, the solicitor, at present away from home on an important case in London so he had asked Vic to stand in and represent the Rotary Club.

"We've had an invitation," announced Vic as he came in from work.

"Well, I hope it's a good one," replied Mrs Spooner.

"Well, let's say it warrants a new frock. How does that sound?"

"Will the queen be there?"

"Not quite that important but we are deputised to meet the new mayor at her inauguration party."

"Shouldn't she be mayoress?"

"No. mayoress is the lady of a male mayor. This lady lakes the job herself so I expect her husband to be mayoress."

"Don't be so daft."

The new frock was a good one and Mrs Spooner felt really on top of the world. This was a far cry from the bacon sandwich that started the whole thing off. The reception was very grand indeed and attended by some very influential people as well as senior officers of the council. They were all eating and drinking merrily when the new mayor came in. Her eye seemed to light on Mrs Spooner straight away and she came over, rather to Vic's surprise.

"Well I never! If it isn't my old enemy, Wendy Blowers. How lovely to see you again."

"Actually, it's not Blowers any more. May I introduce my husband, Vic. Spooner." And she held her hand towards Vic so that the mayor shook hands with him warmly.

Vic was impressed. Very impressed. Wait till he reported back to Jones that his wife and the mayor were on first name terms. That would make him sit up and take notice.

The two ladies chatted for a short time recounting their school days together but the mayor had to circulate and Mrs Spooner was left to fill in the blanks with Vic, at least the bare bones of it.

It was not long before the master of ceremonies announced from the dais, "Ladies and gentlemen. Pray silence for the new mayor, Councillor Mrs Joyce Dixon-Rhudders."

There was a ripple of applause across the room but Mrs Spooner had to cover her face and turn away almost choking.

"What's the matter with you?" hissed Vic as silently as he could.

His wife tried to whisper but that isn't easy when you are trying not to laugh. "I've never heard her full name until now. It sounds like joysticks and rudders."

Vic had to suppress an urge to grin. A couple behind them had overheard Mrs, Spooner's comment and they too were trying not to laugh. Before long, it was being whispered most irreverently from group to group all around the room.

Joyce was paying close attention to her notes describing how she intended to use the mayor's charity this year in support of a children's hospice and how she intended to put the town on the map by making improvements in the town centre area so that people would come from miles around to do their shopping here. It was a serious inaugural address so when she finished and looked to the crowd for mild applause, she was rather surprised to see all of them grinning madly as if she had just said something extremely funny. Some were even having difficulty not laughing out loud.

From that occasion onwards, she was referred to in the town hall as "Old Joysticks", an epitaph which clung to her throughout her term of office. It also presaged a year of blunders and problems which she would not have thought possible.

# Chapter Thirteen

The office of mayor was certainly not everyone's cup of tea. Many councillors of long standing never took that office for several reasons but it was something that Joyce had coveted for years. It carried prestige, which suited Joyce very well and Harold even better because he was able to tell his friends at Westminster that when he came home at weekends, he had to refer to his wife as "Your worship". This got a mild laugh first time, less of a laugh second time and thereafter only bored.

It was customary for the mayor, at the beginning of a term, to pronounce his or her intentions and Joyce had declared herself in support of the hospice as the charity and improvement of the shopping as her civic thing. It was accepted, though never publicised, that the mayor would use personal influence in these matters but provision of personal finance was frowned upon because it could act as a deterrent to future mayoral candidates. Notwithstanding that, everyone knew that it cost a few bob to carry the office for a year.

She was allocated two permanent members of staff plus ancillary use of clerical staff when needed. The most important person was Desmond Quirk, the official ceremonials officer who acted as a personal assistant and Mace Bearer for civic functions. Desmond was experienced, having seen twelve previous mayors through the job. He would be responsible for arranging Joyce's diary, fixing up prestigious meetings and functions and even writing her speeches in many cases. The other member of staff was Ted Brown, a surly little man who was the mayor's chauffeur and that's all. He had been promoted from the general transport pool and considered this job to be the best the council could offer a driver, apart from which he was able to laud it over the other drivers. But he certainly did not intend to be subservient – he was as good as the next man – so he drove the car. If the mayor wanted to get in or out, it could be done perfectly well without him having to open the door like some serf.

Desmond was a brick. Early in the term he had arranged a series of events on a weekday which, it was hoped, would give a start to both of Joyce's projects. The first was a visit to the town centre shopping precinct where a major company was opening a new branch of 'Miss Fitz', the women's outfitters. They wanted to make a special occasion out of the opening so Desmond agreed that the mayor would attend, complete with chain of office on two conditions. Firstly, Miss Fitz would provide secure escort from the mayoral car at the entrance to the shopping centre and back. Second, Miss Fitz would donate £1000 which would go to the children's hospice.

After that, Joyce would be whisked off to lunch at the Rotary Club where she would be able to plead for cash donations to her other pet project which was to provide new Christmas lights for the town so that new customers could be persuaded to come in from surrounding districts. This was something that the traders had to support because the council had decided years ago that public finance for Christmas lights would never exceed what the traders contributed and even then there would be a ceiling.

After lunch she would be taken on to an afternoon meeting of the Women's Institute.

When the day arrived, Joyce was ready. Desmond had written three speeches for her which she had taken home on the previous evening to study. She took a long bath and took her time getting ready so she was pacing up and down impatiently by the time Ted drove up to her front door at 10.30 sharp. It took only about 15 minutes to the shopping precinct which was a grand place with two storeys of car parking over the top but Joyce was to be met at the main entrance where there were forbidding double yellow lines so there would be no chance of there being nowhere to pull up. The managing director of 'Miss Fitz' was awaiting her arrival along with a couple of uniformed tough guys so Joyce put the chain of office around her neck and stepped out as one of the security guards held the door.

Introductions were made and soon the official party was walking through the centre towards the 'Miss Fitz' store. Joyce was beginning to feel a few butterflies in her stomach now but was supremely confident that she had been over everything in her mind so nothing would go wrong.

Back in the car, Ted had 45 minutes to kill and he was dying for a cup of tea. The trouble was that if he left the car here, he would almost certainly get a parking ticket because the council, unwisely in Ted's view, had sub contracted all traffic warden duties to a private concern which might as well have been called the Gestapo. The attitude of the attendants was several degrees worse than uncompromising and they would take great delight in adding the mayor's limo to their list of pinched celebrities if the chance arose. If he so much as got out of the car for a smoke, one of them would surely pounce and then ask, "How was I to know it was a Mayor's car?" It had happened to Ted a couple of years ago and he'd been lucky to keep his job over it. So he drove the car up to the parking deck, collected a ticket from the machine and came down in the lift to go for a cuppa in the caff.

Joyce was shown the new shop, a rectangular, featureless unit, with the sort of fittings she could have seen anywhere but she kept smiling for the sake of the fee. A crowd of passively interested shoppers had gathered when Joyce began her speech and she was not too impressed with their lack of interest in what was being said. Joyce concluded that they were there for the special opening day offers rather that the ceremony so when it came to cutting the tape and declaring the shop open, she was not sorry. As she cut the tape, there was an interruption on the public address system.

"This is a security announcement. Will all personnel please leave the precinct as quickly as possible by the nearest exit. Do not go to the car park floors because the barriers are down. Repeat. This is a security announcement. Will all personnel…"

The P.A. droned on but Joyce had heard enough. In the company of the managing director and the two security men, she made her way towards the main entrance. One of the security men observed that this was standard procedure when a bag of any sort was left unattended and that it happened about once a month. One of the crowd members happened to be Alec Smart, a reporter for the Echo. He had been sent down by his boss and had listened attentively, hoping that somebody would make a slip so that an otherwise dull event might actually produce a readable story so when the security announcement came, he was one whose day started to look brighter.

Meantime, as Ted had finished his cuppa and was on the way out of the caff, he was ushered by security to the opposite end of the precinct and found himself without the mayor's car and about a quarter of a mile away from the mayor. He was not at all pleased. He would now be in big trouble for leaving the car so he'd better think up some excuse.

As Joyce emerged into the open, she immediately noticed that the car was missing. She looked up and down the road but there was no sign of it or of the chauffeur. "Where's the damned car?" she expostulated. It was probably a rhetorical question really because nobody in her party could have the least idea. They all looked up and down the road as well and just as uselessly because there was no car there. A policeman on duty was hailed and seeing the mayoral chain of office came across smartly. "Have you seen the mayor's car?" she asked.

"Yes, ma'am. I watched you arrive in it then it drove off as soon as you had gone inside."

"But it was supposed to be here waiting for me. I've got to get across town to a Rotary Club meeting somehow."

She turned angrily to Alec Smart and snapped, "Stop taking pictures, you idiot, and see if you can't be useful." But Alec was having the time of his life and the last thing he wanted was for the mayor's car to turn up now.

Joyce was beginning to lose her composure completely and the man from 'Miss Fitz' wanted to get rid of her so that he could get back to work. "Can I call you a minicab?" he enquired helpfully. Joyce very nearly gave him a rude answer until it dawned upon her what he meant.

"Oh. Yes please. That would be kind."

He called a cab number on his mobile and reported that there would be a 10-minute wait. "I'm running late as it is," she pleaded. "Can't they do better."

The managing director was as important-sounding as possible. "Look here, old chap. This is an emergency. The cab is required for the mayor."

That seemed to make a difference and the delay was suddenly reduced to three or four minutes. Alec Smart was absolutely in his glory. He might even get front page for this.

When the cab arrived, it was clearly not the best of the fleet but Joyce had no option now. She bade a hasty farewell to her hosts and jumped in the back. It smelt like something between vomit and deodorant so she opened both windows wide and gave the driver the name of the hostelry where the Rotary Club was meeting. And off they went.

Jones had been like a cat on hot bricks all morning because this was the most important day he had endured since becoming president. The members were there in numbers, all at the bar imbibing according to what they expected to be their respective capacities by one o' clock. But the mayor wasn't here yet and Jones knew that if they all had another one, the lunch could easily become a bit raucous. He was pacing up and down outside, having sent a message to the kitchen that the start would be delayed when a tatty green minicab pulled up and out stepped a windswept looking lady wearing about £50000 worth of gold and enamel around her neck.

"Hello," she said. "You must be Mr Jones. I'm the mayor. Sorry to be late but I'll explain later. I must have a couple of minutes in the ladies room before we begin. Oh, and would you mind paying the cab driver. All my money is in the official car and that is missing."

And with that she dashed into the ladies to try to tidy her hair without the usual implements in a handbag. Jones was nonplussed for a second or two, then he paid off the cab and called the members in to lunch. Joyce followed soon after and they all stood at their places ready to sing Grace. Only then did anyone realise that Theodore was not present today and it was he who played the piano to accompany the less than perfect singing. None of the others had any musical knowhow, not even enough to play the two or three chords necessary to get Grace underway. So Jones picked what he thought was a reasonable note and led them in. "Oh Lord and Giver of all good."

The others, a little emboldened by the extra drink, joined in with gusto.

Those who know Rotary Grace will realise that the highest note comes in the penultimate line. Nine out of ten of them couldn't reach it because Jones had pitched it too high so half of them went down an octave and the other half simply missed the note by a semitone or thereabouts, resulting in the most awful cacophony. The last line was drowned in coughs, splutters and even downright laughter. Jones scowled as they sat down.

Throughout lunch, Joyce chatted with Jones and another fellow with one of those north country names ending in bottom. He was an undertaker. It was easy conversation and enabled her to relax a little before addressing this all-male event. She had been told to keep her remarks short and to the point because that was what they were used to and they all had to get back to work. When coffee was being served, Jones stood up and introduced the mayor shortly but correctly. Joyce stood up and unfolded the speech which luckily had been in her pocket and not in her handbag. When she looked at the paper in her hand, her heart sank. It began "Good afternoon ladies. Thank you for inviting me to the WI."

"Oh shit," she muttered audibly enough for Jones to hear. Joyce was absolutely confused, her mind a total blank. For the life of her, she couldn't remember what she was going to say. All she could think about was the things she was going to do to that awful Ted Brown if he ever dared show his face again. In desperation she said, "Sorry to be late. Are there any questions?"

It was a master stroke. This was the shortest after lunch address the Rotary Club had ever known and in view of the late start, it was the right time to do it. There were cheers and applause though Joyce knew not why. The members loved her. One had the temerity to ask, "Your worship. Could you please tell us something about your support staff?" A genuine question genuinely asked.

"As of today," began Joyce in reply, "I'm looking for a new chauffeur." And she briefly explained what had happened in the morning. There were other questions after that and when Jones closed the meeting, everyone felt that it had been a good and useful insight into the working of the mayor's office.

As they filed out, Jones offered Joyce a lift back to the town hall which she accepted in the hope that Brown would at least have returned her handbag even if he had stolen the damned car. When Jones had dropped her off, Joyce suddenly realised that she had intended to persuade the Rotary Club to part with a lot of money towards new Christmas lights. A chance missed. Damn, damn, damn.

# Chapter Fourteen

Ted Brown was on the carpet. The mayor demanded to know why he had departed with the car against her specific instructions.

"It wasn't my fault," he tried. "When the security warning came the police moved me on to make way for service vehicles."

"That's a lie," Joyce almost shouted but kept her composure, so well that it unnerved Ted. "I asked the police about your movements and they made it clear that you moved off as soon as I was out of sight. Not only that but your record shows that you've done this before. So I'm having you posted back to the driving pool."

"You can't do that."

"Well, as a matter of fact I can and I do. I want my term of office to go with a bang. I won't have it spoiled by the likes of you."

Ted went out in a foul mood and left the mayor in another. He would go back to driving a Meals on Wheels van or a dustcart and serve him right. But Ted was a man who carried a grudge.

Next day, Joyce got up feeling a lot better, as if she had started to take control of her life again. Her high spirits were short lived when someone brought in the local paper.

Mrs Spooner also read the local paper over breakfast, at least she would have done but couldn't get past the front page. It wasn't much of a story at all but the art of the tabloid reporter is to make a story out of nothing, the last word in spin doctoring. So with a photograph of Joyce not at her best and a banner headline reading "JOYSTICKS LOSES LIMO", there wasn't much room to print the very few facts that Alec smart had discovered. Nevertheless, he had contrived, without justification, to brand the mayor an idiot or worse. Mrs Spooner telephoned the mayor's office and was eventually put through to Joyce.

"Wendy. How nice to hear from someone who isn't going to gloat over my misfortune. What can I do for you?"

"You can put your chain of office in the safe, tell them in the office that you won't be back until 3 and then walk outside. I'll pick you up and take you to lunch."

"Wendy, that's a splendid offer from the first sane person I've spoken to all day. You're on."

The two old enemies, now grown up, got on far better now than ever they used to and the lunch was an enjoyable interlude. Mrs Spooner found out that Joyce had been having an unhappy time of it most days and wished she had never taken the job on but she would see it through even though the mayor's charity was looking about the worst on record and as far as the Christmas lights were concerned, it looked as though she would have no more than about £5000 to spend which would go practically nowhere. And she still had to find a new chauffeur.

At the next council meeting, it was agreed that the post should be advertised internally in case any other drivers were interested. Also it was agreed that the post should be upgraded to chauffeur and body guard because there were times when security was important. After all, there had been the egg throwing incident a couple of years back and the chain of office was a valuable piece of jewellery. So a notice was posted. There were two replies, one from Arnold Walker whose wife urged him to apply because it would be better for her to describe her husband as a mayor's chauffeur than a dustcart driver. The other applicant was Cuthbert Bermingham known to his friends on the carts as Cuff. He was a dreamer and bodybuilder in his spare time. To be a bodyguard was everything that Cuff had dreamed of. He had seen all the American movies with the FBI bodyguards running alongside the president's Limo, protecting him with their own bodies. Yes, this was the job for him. Both applicants had been interviewed by Des Quirk but Joyce wanted to see them personally.

Cuff came in first. He was dressed in a dark suit and tie, crisp white shirt and Ray Bands, trailing a hint of Old Spice. Arnold came in second wearing jeans, tee shirt and a brown leather sleeveless body warmer, trailing a hint of civic amenity depot. There was no contest. Cuthbert was appointed.

He proved to be everything that Ted had not been. He was smart and attentive and, in a way, added a touch of dignity to the office by always treating Joyce with deference and not questioning her orders. Mind you, there were times when she thought he might be going a little over the top but that really didn't matter. Joyce began to think things were looking up.

Joyce was doubly convinced of this when she next met Mrs Spooner for what had become a regular lunch thing. Mrs Spooner had mentioned at home that Joyce had fallen far short of target in her fund-raising effort for new Christmas lights and Vic had mentioned it at Rotary lunch one day. It had been Phil Collins who said that he had a brother working for Brighton Corporation and as they regularly updated their sea front lighting display, there was usually a warehouse full of second-hand lights which were available at knock down prices. Mrs Spooner suggested that Joyce and Phil might take a day out together at the seaside to investigate.

It turned out to be better than ever Joyce could have imagined. It was like visiting an Aladdin's cave with lights of every shape and size except for actual Christmas motifs. So by avoiding the obviously unsuitable and seeing the potential of converting a gnome into a Santa quite easily, Joyce was able to buy for her £5000 a whole heap of exotic coloured lights, enough to light up the town centre without having to use any of the ordinary street lights. This would show them.

The town council was rather cool about her second-hand lights project and wouldn't agree to any extra expenditure for things like repainting them or putting them up but other people in town were much more helpful. Vic organised some free aid from club members in painting white beards on red gnomes and such like, Desmond Quirk organised a band of volunteer council workers to put them all up and the borough engineer undertook to test them and wire them up for a grand switching on ceremony.

Joyce herself organised other things. First of all, she went to the local theatre where Peter Pablo, the heart throb soap opera star, was playing in panto and persuaded him to do the official switching on. He agreed because advance bookings were not doing too well and the first Friday in December would be a good time to plug the show and to let his adoring public see him in the flesh. Actually, he would be in costume because it would have to be 6 o'clock, between the matinee and the evening performance. Joyce had to promise him that it would be a grand occasion so secretly, at her own expense, she hired an open landau and two horses to take the official switching on party from the car park to the dais where the red handle would be. Carruthers had, unusually for him, offered to build a six-foot-high platform with a stairway so that the whole party could be seen by the crowds which would gather in market square. The big department store had agreed to the use of their forecourt which had a wide awning over the pavement about 16 feet above ground so if the weather should be inclement, the official party would remain sheltered even if they got soaked in the open landau on the way. And to cap it all, Harold was coming down from Westminster to witness the spectacle.

The council volunteers worked hard, after hours, to get the lights up. Nobody really noticed that Ted Brown was part of the volunteer group or if they did, thought not to question his motives for being there. He didn't ever do anything for nothing and hadn't been turning over new leaves, that's for sure. If Joyce had noticed, she would have been very suspicious. She would have been even more suspicious if she had seen him on the top of the awning on the afternoon before switching on but the duty policeman, who knew Ted vaguely, did notice but saw no significance in it. After all he was wearing one of the council's reflective waistcoats so he was obviously on official business.

It was arranged that the official car with the mayor would drive to the car park at the back of the theatre where the carriage would be waiting for the switching on party. They would then proceed by open carriage through the town centre to the platform. A stable lass who knew the horses would walk at their head. The problem was with Cuff. As bodyguard, he would have to stay with the mayor but in his dark suit, he would look out of place because Joyce intended to dress up in style, to match, and perhaps impress, Peter Pablo. The only costume that could be located big enough for Cuff's 16-stone body was for a postillion. Cuff declined the offer of a ride on the lead horse and decided to walk at the back where he could keep a weather eye open for potential trouble. As he said, "You can't be too careful."

On the big day, the borough engineer and his team were on parade before daybreak to test and make the final connection to the big red lever on the platform. They certainly looked magnificent to the few people who were around at that hour. In the afternoon, Harold arrived and wished his wife good luck and then arranged to meet Vic and Mrs Spooner for the grand show. Joyce dressed in her fancy costume in good time for Cuff to pick her up in the Limo. Then they picked up Peter Pablo and climbed into the waiting landau. As they rode through the town centre, they certainly attracted a lot of attention, at least Peter Pablo did, and Joyce gladly shared the adulation. Desmond Quirk had made all the mundane arrangements like policing and ambulance stand by and he himself, dressed in the formal tail coat and breeches of the Mace Bearer, waited at the platform for the party to arrive.

There must have been over 1000 people in the square including, at the back, Harold and Vic and Mrs Spooner. They stood in a pub doorway where Harold was dispensing whiskey and hospitality to his electorate. The coach reached the steps and they all got out and mounted the platform to great cheers. Cuff, for his part had been busily watching the crowd for signs of danger. When the coach stopped, he was anxious to make sure that the horses didn't wander off because he didn't, for one minute, believe that the little girl leading them could possibly stop two horses from doing just as they pleased. Not knowing about the primitive braking systems for horse drawn vehicles, he thought that he had better take the heavy shoe thing on a chain and wrap it around the newel post of the steps. Then he took up his station immediately behind the mayor where he could watch the crowd and protect her back. This was really being a good bodyguard. He'd show them.

Peter Pablo got his commercial in and entranced the crowd for ten minutes before the countdown began. Ten, nine, eight, seven, six, five, four, three, two, one, zero. Peter pulled the red handle towards him. Simultaneously the streetlights were doused and Joyce's new lights came on. They were absolutely magnificent for a second or so because something else happened at the same time. It was Ted's revenge. With a mighty whoosh a rocket was launched automatically from the top of the awning right above the platform party. Cuff knew that his moment had come. This was clearly an attack on the mayor so, regardless of his own safety, he hurled his sixteen stones forward, bringing the mayor to the floor where he protected her with his body. In doing so, the mayor's chain caught around the red lever and pulled it forward again so that the town was plunged into inky blackness. The whoosh of the rocket also disturbed about 50000 pigeons which had bedded down for the night and sent them flying around in circles wondering what would happen next. The assembled crowd looked towards the sky. If they were expecting the rocket to produce a great display of colour, they were mistaken because all they got was an ear-splitting explosion and a blinding flash. The explosion so terrified the circling pigeons that their bowels turned to water above a sea of upturned faces. The horses, calm so far, suddenly bolted in terror leaving the little girl in a heap on the floor and taking with them the landau and the staircase leading to the platform. In the crowd, children cried for their mothers and young men groped around indiscriminately for their young women. It was the cool-headed Desmond who restored order, simply by stepping forward and pulling the red handle back to the on position. Then it was that the crowd saw what they had all been splattered with.

Harold stepped outside the pub and asked what was going on. The ambulance team had got to the platform and were attending to Joyce as she recovered her dignity following Cuff's rugby tackle. The police were trying to recover the bolting horses and the crowd was beginning to disperse in an ugly mood.

Next morning, Mrs Spooner went to the hospital to console her new-found friend, carrying a large bunch of flowers. There was no lasting damage and Joyce had only been kept in for observation but the friendship of Mrs Spooner helped to soften the disappointment of the previous night's disaster. On the way out, Mrs Spooner bumped into Rev Thornthwaite going in.

"Hello Theo. Have you come to visit the mayor?"

"Actually no. I'm here in my capacity as chaplain to the Council Workers Union," he replied. "I'm visiting someone called Ted Brown."

"Oh! What's he done then?"

"I'm really not sure. I'm told that he was run down by a horse and cart or something but I can hardly believe that."

"Theo, you must have been away."

"Yes. How did you know? I only got back this morning."

# Chapter Fifteen

It was well into the new year before Wendy and Joyce could resume their lunchtime meetings. Mrs Spooner hardy knew what mood to expect to find her friend in but she didn't expect the grey gloom which Joyce bore on her face and in the way she held herself.

"Whatever is this job doing to you?" she asked, rather taken aback.

"You wouldn't believe if I told you," she replied.

"Try me. I can listen."

"Well. Ted Brown has decided to sue for damage and suffering caused by a runaway horse and cart. The council say that they didn't authorise the bloody thing so if he succeeds, I'll be surcharged. How's that for starters?"

Mrs Spooner was so angry that a hard-working mayor could be treated so badly when she had been acting in the best interests of the town all the time. "That's outrageous. What are you doing about it?"

"Nothing. I haven't any fight left in me."

"Come on. That's no good. What do the police say about the rocket. Surely the person who put that there is responsible, not you."

"You could be right but I just don't know where to start."

"We'll start by pulling a few strings. I'll get Vic to speak to the Rotary man on the police liaison committee and you ask that Desmond fellow to find out who was on the working party. Then we can compare notes."

It took little effort to discover that Ted had been on the working party, that he had a brother working in the fireworks factory out of town and that a policeman had seen Ted on top of the awning. Desmond discovered that Ted's time sheet showed him booking off at 2 pm whereas the policeman went off duty at 1 pm. Vic and Mrs Spooner confronted Ted with this evidence and he withdrew his claim unconditionally. When Joyce heard what they had done, she was so full of gratitude that she persuaded Harold to take the Spooners out for a first-class meal. Harold raised no objection because that was the sort of thing he did best of all so he made a reservation at the Majestic.

The head waiter and the wine waiter were exceedingly impressed that the local MP and the mayor were bringing their special guests to the Majestic and were at great pains to make sure that the event would enhance the reputation of their establishment. A table was set in a prominent position where everyone would be able to see the quality of the clientele. The staff were almost lined up in salute when the mayoral Limousine pulled up outside, then their faces dropped as first Mrs Spooner and then Vic climbed out, followed by the mayor and the MP. The head waiter was at a total loss. Technically, the Spooners were barred but he couldn't possibly exclude them in these circumstances. So nothing was said.

Vic greeted the head waiter cheerfully, "Hello, old chap. Nice to see you again." It was like a knife going in.

"And I'm pleased to see you too, sir, in such august company."

"Ah! So you're known here," said Harold. "That's useful. We should be able to get the best champagne if they know you." He looked at the wine waiter pointedly. "Make sure you have a bottle of the best ready when I give you the word, OK."

"Certainly, sir," he replied, all the time wondering what Vic would do with it this time.

The meal went very well indeed, not a single hitch in spite of the fact that the staff were on tenterhooks all the time. Eventually Harold called for the champagne and the wine waiter was most careful to place the wine bucket well out of reach on an unoccupied table. The champagne drinking went without a hitch as well so when they all got up to leave, it was plain to see the looks of relief on the faces of the staff.

As they went down the steps to the street, Vic half turned to wave a cheery, "Goodbye and thanks very much." It was the discarded swizzle burger that caused the trouble, or to be more precise, the mayo between the reconstituted meat and the reconstituted cheese. As Vic trod on it, there was no friction at all and down he went on the steps, catching his head such a blow as to render him unconscious. In an instant, Mrs Spooner was down on hands and knees at Vic's side, doing what she had learned in the girl guides, loosen tight clothing about the neck. Joyce was back inside like lightning. Without so much as a by your leave, she grabbed the telephone from the receptionist who was taking a booking, cut off the call and dialled 999. When answered, she was heard to say, "This is the mayor. I want an ambulance to the Majestic quicker than you have ever done it before." There was a lull while someone at the other end said something and Joyce's face clouded.

"Yes, it is old Joysticks," she thundered. "And if you don't believe it, you will find out to your cost."

As it happened, the ambulance took a little over four minutes but it seemed like longer. People trying to leave the restaurant couldn't get out and those arriving couldn't get in. A crowd soon gathered muttering things about posh people getting drunk in posh places. The head waiter was having something like apoplexy trying to placate customers each side of the prostrate Vic and Mrs Spooner was cradling his bleeding head.

He was soon carried into the ambulance and his wife was allowed to travel to hospital with him. At the accident and emergency department, Mrs Spooner was asked to wait while the ambulance men wheeled Vic into a curtained cubicle, one of about nine, for examination. A doctor and a nurse pushing an instrument trolley soon followed pulling the curtain across behind them.

The doctor looked at the cut on Vic's head, then shone a torch into his eyes and pronounced, "Not much wrong with this one. I'd better take his blood pressure then I'll clean the cut up. See if you can get his jacket off, will you?"

The doctor turned to the trolley to set up the sphygmomanometer while the nurse slipped one of Vic's arms out of his sleeve then grasped him round the neck to lift him so as to pass the coat underneath him. Vic came to, albeit still semi dazed, and gazed into the beautiful eyes of Briony Freshwater. The last time she had done this to him, he remembered, she had been naked. Vic thought, *It must be my birthday. And she's dressed in a nurse's suit. Yippee,* and he made a grab for the non-existent Velcro. This manoeuvre was, not surprisingly, misunderstood. Briony squealed and jumped back crashing into the doctor as he leaned over the trolley. The doctor lost his balance and started to pitch forward, reaching out for the dividing curtain to steady himself. His 15 stone was too much. The doctor, the trolley and the curtain all came crashing down together exposing the bare behind of a lady in the next compartment awaiting a pain-killing injection. Indignantly, the lady sat up and stared at Vic whose face was one of surprise and astonishment. "Mrs Carruthers," he exclaimed. "Fancy seeing you."

At the scream and the crash, Mrs Spooner came dashing in to see what had gone wrong. She came face to face with Briony.

"Hallo, love," she said. "I see you didn't give up the day job then."

# Chapter Sixteen

Gladys Finnegan wasn't from these parts. As a matter of fact, she hadn't always been Gladys Finnegan. She was born and registered as Gladys Green, a name she came to detest as she got to that age where such matters are important. She was the only daughter of a business couple who managed to produce a baby rather late in life and quite against anything that they then wanted. As a consequence, Gladys got to know the nannies and the aux pairs rather better than she knew her parents. She went to boarding school when old enough and tended to come home less and less frequently in the school holidays.

She grew up to be a good-looking, young and confident woman but was never academically up to much. Somehow, she thought that a good marriage would provide for her. When an Irishman called Finnegan came into her life, she was swept off her feet. She fell for his Irish charm completely, married him without question and for just over two years she was totally happy and completely secure. Then one day another Irishman came, an older more serious man, who engaged Finnegan in deep and serious conversation. Then he was gone, leaving Gladys alone and unhappy, not even aware where he had gone. It took many months for Gladys to come to terms with the fact that she had been deserted, left with what? Some memories, a few debts and a name. She gradually began to hate Finnegan for deserting her but decided to keep the only thing that was worthwhile, that is, the name. Gladys Finnegan was a damned sight better than Gladys Green. At least it sounded like a name rather than sounding like a London suburb.

Gladys was reluctant to go to her parents for help even though she knew that they had a lot of money and would be glad to see that she was financially secure. She had no qualifications so there wasn't much she could do and somewhat in desperation she became a tele-salesperson, phoning people all day and every day to try selling them double glazing. The thing was, she was good at it, very good in fact and within two years had been promoted to training other tele-salespersons to be as good as she was. The increase in salary that went with the training job made a big difference and she began to recover her independence and her confidence but the experience with Finnegan had changed her. She had become hardened in a subtle way. She was determined never to let another man get so close to her because she believed that was the only way that she could be certain to avoid that awful pain again. On the other hand, she did not intend to remain celibate for the rest of her days. So from time to time, when the need arose, she would select a suitable man, have her wicked way with him and then drop him before things got serious. She took care to make sure that she didn't reveal her identity to these men so there would be no pursuit when the time came to call a halt.

For two or three years, Gladys was content with the training job but by now she was one of the longest standing members of the company and was looking for something better. Not surprisingly, her employer wanted to keep her where she was but Gladys, by now, had a better working knowledge of double glazing than many of the operatives who installed the stuff so when Twinkleglaze advertised for a manager for a new shop in a new town, she applied. The interview was interesting because the company hadn't expected a woman to apply for the job and she had only been put on the shortlist so that they could see what kind of a tough cookie had the temerity to apply for a job in such a tough line. But Gladys impressed them with her depth of knowledge on the subject and for her uncompromising attitude to controlling the installers. So they put her on three months trial.

Gladys was delighted. Her first job had been a little unfortunate because the poor old lady who had been her first customer had dropped down dead the day after the work was completed. But it had been a good job, well-executed and had given her the chance to let the various odd builders who did the installation work that Gladys Finnegan would not accept shoddy work, undue delay or bad language on site. They gradually came to see that her attitude was best because, so long as they behaved, they had a constant stream of work and regular payment. It saved them worrying.

# Chapter Seventeen

Penny and Ben were to be married. Mrs Spooner was very excited about the prospect and Vic thought it was about time. There was obviously a lot of talk about the arrangements and so forth but when it came down to it, it was Penny's day and only she would decide what would happen. Ben said that he didn't really want a high-profile wedding which might come to the attention of the likes of Jacko and other undesirables from his past but was happy for it to be a proper church ceremony. Penny respected this view so it was decreed by her that the wedding would be in church with the service taken by Theodore Thornthwaite. It would be family and close friends only and afterwards there would be a wedding breakfast in the old-fashioned way with everyone sitting down at table. There would not be a disco for the more distant hangers on.

The family considered and rejected the Majestic on the grounds of cost and if the management of the Majestic had known that, they would have been very pleased. Instead, Phil Simmonds of the Rotary Club was kind enough to book the Golf Club. He was on the committee and had bit of clout up there. They could lay on excellent food and being a private club, there would be no chance of interruption by the likes of Carruthers. He had been objectionable enough already, making his snide remarks about jailbirds marrying into Vic's wealth. Vic was so used to these remarks by now that he was able to ignore them.

The day went without incident. They could have gone to the Majestic after all.

Ben and Penny had bought a house on the edge of town in a pleasant neighbourhood. It had been in a dilapidated condition but with the resources of Spooner and Lanes at his disposal, it had been turned into a very nice home by the time Penny was carried across the threshold. Next door was a young couple, Elise and Raymond with a young baby. Penny and Elise soon became very good friends.

Elise had started life as Elsie in an East London suburb, the second oldest in a family with seven children. It was a warm family with lots of laughter but never any money. Father worked in the docks and had work most weeks but sometimes none at all. Mother had to turn out and work sometimes and both parents longed for the day when the kids would be old enough to go to work to add a bit of financial security to the family. When her elder sister was 15, she left school and got a job at the car plant. She got her first pay packet on the Friday, gave a bit of keep to her mother and then went out on the binge. By Monday morning, she was broke and back at the car plant.

Elsie decided that this was not for her. She was coming up to 14 and would be next for the slaughter unless she did something about it but she had never bothered with school work and hadn't a hope in hell of getting any decent exam results. One day at school, when she was particularly morose, her form mistress asked what was troubling her.

"Well, Miss. I've got about a year left at school before I have to follow my sister into the car plant and the idea terrifies me. What can I do?"

The teacher was a realist and knew that a lecture about hard work would not do here. This girl was clever without being academically inclined, a fairly common circumstance in this part of the country. So she began. "Can I be perfectly frank without upsetting you, Elsie?"

"I should think so, Miss," was the cautious reply.

"Right then. Elsie, you have a pretty face, an alert mind and a sense of humour, but when you open your mouth, you sound like a squawking parrot. The cockney accent will spoil your chances of doing well more certainly than the lack of exam passes so I recommend you concentrate on that."

"How do you mean – like go to elocution lessons or something?"

"No, no. Nothing that drastic. If you try to speak like the queen, you'll never make it. All you need to do is to start pronouncing your Ts, stop dropping your aitches and get those vowel sounds nearer to mine. Just listen to the radio and try to copy the people who speak reasonably but whatever you do, don't try to be posh."

"How will that help, Miss?"

"It might enable you to get a better job than you deserve. So think on."

"Blimey, Miss, that ain't going to be easy."

But Elsie took those words to heart and spent hours in the bedroom every evening quietly practising. As well as improving her diction, she also found that by speaking less loudly, she began to sound, if not a bit refined, then certainly a lot less common. It cost her some friendships and made her a bit of an outcast at school but that only served to tell Elsie that she had a streak of determination or even ruthlessness that she didn't know she had. When it came to leaving school, she applied for a job as filing clerk in the council offices. It didn't pay a fabulous amount but there was a day release opportunity which meant that she could go to commercial college and learn a few other things.

Elsie smiled and charmed her way through an interview and got the job even though she was by no means the most able applicant. Then she set about making the most of the opportunity.

By the time she was 19, Elsie had worked her way up in the town hall and gained some useful certificates in typing, book keeping and general secretarial duties and felt able to spread her wings to an environment where she might come into contact with suitable husband material. The average male of the town hall was not to her liking and unlikely ever to earn enough to support the lifestyle that Elsie had in mind. So she looked around at the adverts and other opportunities and eventually applied for and secured a minor secretarial post in a finance house. It was miles away from London, a totally new start in a new locality, so she took the opportunity to accidentally misspell her name. That was when Elsie disappeared and Elise was born. It sounded a hundred times better. Now she could set about changing the surname as well.

In her new office, it didn't take Elise very long to size up the men. She decided that Raymond Goodyear was a worthwhile target for a number of reasons. Firstly, Elise Goodyear sounded quite nice, secondly Raymond was a very handsome young man and thirdly, she judged that he was destined for high office. If she could hang onto him for about

7 years, he would be high enough up the ladder of success to be worth divorcing for financial reasons. On the downside, he was rather pompous in some ways and tended to look down on the womenfolk, as he called them as, not infrequently, he told everyone how good he was at understanding the fair sex. "I can read a woman's mind like a book," he was once, or twice, heard to boast.

Elise's face and wiles soon had him trapped in spite of his protestations that he had the matter well under control. But she had him up the aisle within a year of marking him.

Once married, Elise decided that it wouldn't be proper for her to work in the same firm as Raymond and he agreed, so she gave up her job and started getting friendly with her neighbours, especially Penny, who was herself spending a little less time at work now that Spooner and Lanes were doing so well. So when Elise mentioned that she was pregnant, Penny was delighted and took a great interest in the forthcoming event. Elise and Raymond had been married for nearly two years by then and Penny thought it was a good time to start. She would have to talk to Ben. There was no question of Elise going back to work when the baby actually arrived and Raymond was careful to tell one and all that it was his decision to see that his little wife stayed home quite properly to look after home and baby.

But as the baby got a little bigger and more of a demand on mother, Raymond started to have a wandering eye, even worse, he had wandering thoughts. It had long been the practise that the men in Raymond's department would lunch in the office all through the week but on Fridays the men would all go off together to a wine bar leaving the office in charge of the 'fairer sex'. Raymond always referred to them thus on a Friday to please them he told his colleagues. "You see, it's psychology, makes them feel important you know. When you understand women like I do, it comes as second nature."

His male colleagues made no comment simply because Raymond was senior to them and didn't take kindly to other points of view. But it didn't stop them thinking that he knew less that he made out.

It was during one of these Friday Male Bonding lunches that Raymond noticed an auburn-haired woman giving him the eye. Raymond was flattered but understood that it must be difficult for the lady if she had spotted him and liked what she saw. The trouble was that she was there again on the following Friday, but this time not just giving him the eye, but smiling an invitation. He was unable to resist and made a point of being up at the bar beside her when she was buying a drink so that he could chat her up. They fell into conversation and 'fore you could say Jack Robinson, she was suggesting that they meet one evening soon to get better acquainted. This was the beginning of an affair.

Elise was at home preparing to bake a pie when the phone call came. It was Raymond. "Hello darling. What are you doing?"

Elise was immediately on her guard. Raymond had never before cared what she was up to while he was at work so why now? "I'm making pastry if you must know. Why, what's up?"

"Oh, nothing important. It's just that a rush job has come up and the big boss thinks I'm the only one capable of doing it so I'll be working late tonight."

"What shall I do with this pie then?"

"Well, I'm afraid I'll have to miss out on that one. I'll snatch a bite here and then get on. I could be quite late so don't wait up."

"I'll see you in the morning then I suppose."

"Yes. Bye love."

And that was it. Elise knew with all the certainty of the female instinct that Raymond was lying and she didn't like that at all. It might be something not serious but she would be watching like a hawk.

On the following Friday morning, he announced over breakfast that he would be late again that night. "It's the same job actually. I can see this taking a while yet to get it finished," he offered a little diffidently.

"Well, I daresay the big boss will be giving you a big bonus for this one, won't he?" she queried without trying to hide the scorn in her voice.

"Oh absolutely," he replied.

Elsie idly thought that "absolutely" in that context was quite meaningless as indeed it was in most of its current usage. But that wasn't the real point. Elise was now convinced that Raymond was playing away and that was not how she wanted things to turn out. It was going to take another 4 years before he would be earning enough to be worth divorcing so she had to think of a way to get him back. That wasn't going to be easy.

During the succeeding week, she was having afternoon tea with Penny and was not her usual self. Penny asked what was wrong.

"Since you ask," Elise responded a little tartly, "Raymond is having an affair." Penny was taken aback and no mistake.

"Are you sure?"

"Penny love, I truly hope that it never happens to you but if it does, you will know as certainly as I do."

"Who with?" asked Penny, eschewing the more correct 'with whom' because it sounded daft.

"That I don't know and I think I would rather not know who she is, thank you."

"Do you intend to do anything about it?" Penny was getting curious because Elise didn't seem sufficiently upset to her way of thinking.

"One thing is certain. I will not confront him with the fact that I know because that might force him into making a choice. I want him back. I don't want him to have an option."

"Well, at least that is positive," said Penny. "Have you any ideas?"

"Not yet but I'm working on it."

"Why not warn off the other woman?" asked Penny.

"Because I don't want to know who she is or anything about her I suppose."

"I'll think about that and let you know. There's always the chance that it will fizzle out, you know."

It didn't fizzle out and after four lonely Friday evenings, Elise was beginning to think that it wasn't going to. Raymond, on the other hand, was beginning to think he had got away with it for long enough so he intended to bring it to an end. That wouldn't be difficult because he had told the other woman nothing about himself, not even his real name, so all he needed to do was to change his Friday lunch venue and that would be that. Little did he realise that the other woman was having the same thoughts. It had gone on long enough. She had enjoyed it but it must end before trouble started because she was convinced that he was a married man and his wife wouldn't stay out of the picture forever. She had told him nothing about herself, not even her real name, so all she had to do was change her Friday lunch venue and that would be that.

Matters came to a head when Penny persuaded Elise to let her follow Raymond one Friday to see whether she could deliver an anonymous warning. Raymond wasn't difficult to follow but Penny was a bit surprised when he drove up to the by-pass service station and parked outside a little chef/ Not a romantic venue she would have thought. Penny waited inconspicuously until another car came up and a woman got out to join Raymond. They disappeared into the Travel lodge together. Then Elsie slipped a note under the woman's windscreen wiper. "You have been marked. Leave him alone."

Penny was pleased with her work but would have been less pleased had she known that each of the two contenders had decided that this would be the last time. So when Raymond came home at a proper time on the following Friday and announced that the big job was completed, Elise was delighted and Penny wanted to take all the credit. Raymond, on the other hand, thought that he had got away with it. He just didn't know that the cruel hand of fate was waiting to give him one in the eye.

For the next three weeks, Elise made no mention of the big job but at the end of the month when Raymond's pay cheque was due, she decided to bring the matter up. She never saw Raymond's pay cheques because pay was a man thing, not a girlie thing, so she wouldn't have known how the current one compared with any other one but she asked, for fun really, whether the bonus had been worthwhile. "It was much as I had expected," he ventured with a note of caution in his voice.

"Well, in that case perhaps we can now have the double glazing put in at the front. It will make such a difference to the level of street noise and you know it sometimes wakes the baby."

Raymond recognised the trap. Up until now he had always said that double glazing wasn't necessary but if he said no again, there would be questions about the amount of the bonus and that might get him into deep water. He supposed he could find the money for it so he chose the safe path. Anyway, it was a good thing to butter up the little lady from time to time.

"What a good idea," was his surprising reply. "I'll get someone round to give us an estimate."

It was Elise's birthday and in the afternoon, Penny had gone round with a card and a little present. The two ladies had tea together and got to chatting when there was a ring at the doorbell. Elise went.

"Hello," said the visitor. "I'm Gladys Finnegan from Twinkleglaze. I've come about the windows." Elise judged her to be a pleasant person, probably capable as well and not at all bad-looking.

"Come in," she said, "I've been expecting you."

After the usual pleasantries, Gladys was left to do her measuring up while the others carried on talking.

When Gladys had finished, Penny was also ready to go because she had to get Ben's dinner on. So Elise bade Gladys farewell and remained chatting with Penny a little longer, gradually moving down the garden path as they talked.

Gladys got into her car and sat with her clipboard on the steering wheel as she carefully checked to make sure that she had all the information that she would need. As it was Elise's birthday, Raymond was coming home early. The car was in for a service so he was on the bus today. He had bought a bunch of flowers in town and had an awful job getting them back intact. Raymond was no good at holding flowers as indeed are most men. If he cradled them in the crook of his arm, it looked as though he was carrying a baby. If he held them upright, they looked quite stupid and bridelike and if he held them down by his side they got mashed by passers-by. When he got off the bus, he went into the off license and bought a bottle of Elsie's favourite wine then set off towards the house with flowers aloft in one hand and a plastic carrier bag in the other.

Gladys looked up from her clipboard and saw Raymond coming. Her blood ran cold as she recognised him. "How the hell did he find out that I would be here today? Why the hell didn't he take the hint when I stopped seeing him? What the hell was he doing bringing me flowers and wine? He must be nuts."

Raymond looked up and saw Gladys at about the same moment that he himself had been spotted.

"What the hell is she doing here? Why can't she resist me? How the hell did she find out where I live? Has she come here to stir up trouble?"

All these questions and more raced through the two minds. When Raymond reached the car, he leaned over and, rather clumsily, opened the door of the car just as Elise and Penny arrived at the garden gate behind him.

"What brings you to these parts?" Raymond asked, wondering how best he could get rid of her.

"As if you didn't know," Gladys stormed. "It's no good you coming chasing after me with flowers and wine. It's finished. Understand? And if you come chasing after me again, I'll have you arrested for stalking." And with that she reached across and grabbed the door and slammed it shut so violently that it neatly took all the flower heads off leaving Raymond with a bunch of stalks. As she drove off at a furious pace, Raymond stepped back smartly into a lamp post whereat there was the unmistakable sound of breaking glass.

Raymond turned towards the house and was astonished to see Elise and Penny standing there, jaws dropped and eyes wide with astonishment at the coincidence that they had just witnessed. Elise looked at Raymond standing there with a bunch of flower stalks in one hand and in the other, a carrier bag dripping red wine into his left shoe. What a sight! She had a feeling in the pit of her stomach which was making its way rapidly up through her entire body until it reached her face where it was manifested, first as a smile, then as a chuckle and finally as absolutely helpless laughter. Elise's laughter was infectious and before she knew it, Penny had joined in. The two women, with tears running down their faces, clung together in paroxysms of unbridled mirth while Raymond stood there, po-faced and quite unable to see anything funny at all. And so they remained for long minutes before the laughter subsided to occasional sobs. Raymond was first to speak. "What was all that about?" he asked in all innocence.

Which was all that was needed to set the two women off laughing all over again.

Raymond pushed past them impatiently, walked through the gate and down the sideway to the back door. On the way he dumped the flower stalks and the broken wine bottle in the dustbin and slammed the lid down with a crash. Then he took off his coat and stomped off upstairs to his study.

"Women," he muttered to himself. "Just when you think you understand their little minds, you discover that you really know nothing at all."

# Chapter Eighteen

Life in the Goodyear household was changing. The embarrassing incident with Gladys Finnegan at the garden gate had a profound effect upon Raymond, especially when he thought about it and concluded that he had never really understood the female mind from the start. So much of his power had been sheer illusion. The bush telegraph, being what it is, didn't spare him in the least because it was soon all round the office that he had been ticked off publicly by some tart he had picked up in a wine bar.

This lack of confidence found its way into his work output and soon his figures were not doing as well as they should. Raymond recognised this but something in him had changed and it simply didn't bother him as it once would have done. It was inevitable that the boss called him in for a pep talk.

"Raymond, my boy. Everything all right at home?" It was a question although the boss didn't really care what the answer was.

"Yes. Fine," said Raymond. "Why d'you ask?" although he knew damn well.

"Your figures are not, how shall I say," he paused in mid-sentence so Raymond finished it for him.

"Good enough," he assisted.

"Yes, you have it," replied the Boss. "Can you see any reason for this?"

Raymond could but wasn't going to speak his mind. The fact was that he had become sick and tired of selling financial services because it was totally uncreative. It was the same old routine, day in day out, tell the punter the old story and get him to sign up for the rest of his life. Raymond wasn't going to make it easy for the boss so he said.

"People are getting wiser and have far greater access to information these days."

"Now Raymond that can't be true, can it?" he began. "The man on the Clapham Omnibus," he began. Raymond groaned inwardly at the reference because it looked like being one of the boss's more excruciating lectures. "The man on the Clapham Omnibus is lost and bewildered in a sea of financial services, tax advantages, special pension schemes and a thousand pitfalls. It's your job to show him the way to go and then sign him up. Am I not correct in this?"

"In this day and age," countered Raymond, "the man on the Clapham omnibus knows exactly where he is going by looking at the destination board."

"I'm sorry, Raymond. That's a little too profound for me."

But the writing was on the wall. A month or two later Raymond was invited to take a redundancy package in terms which he couldn't have refused even if he had wanted to but it suited him very well. He was such a changed man that he welcomed the opportunity to materially change his life. He didn't know how but change there would certainly be.

For the first week or two, he found plenty to occupy him but Elise couldn't help noticing that applying for jobs was not one of them. When it got to the fourth week, Elise was getting worried. She had to admit that Raymond was relaxed and pleasant, he had bonded with their baby daughter quite splendidly and was happy to do whatever the little girl needed. When she mentioned finding a job, she was surprised at his response. "I haven't decided what to do yet. I know for certain that I will never again work in a stuffy office dealing with impersonal things like money. It leaves a dissatisfaction which I can't explain."

Elise thought for a while. "We must do something to produce income because your redundancy money won't last for ever. Penny next door had often offered me a bit of secretarial work for her father's firm. It won't pay a lot but it could lead to better things. We'd need to get a computer and I don't mind shutting myself up in the little bedroom."

Surprisingly, Raymond agreed. This would never have satisfied the old Raymond. Elise was well aware that when she married him, long-term security was of paramount importance. That seemed to be out of the window now but somehow she didn't mind. There was something about the new Raymond that she liked.

So Elise acquired a computer and started typing specifications, a strange new language to her. It was time-consuming at first because Elise was determined never to send back substandard work. Penny managed to get a few jobs from other contacts and Elise placed an advertisement in the local paper. Gradually the work started to come in and soon she was working a full 8-hour day. Raymond kept the house clean, kept the baby fed and clean, even started to do the weekly shopping. He was a happy man. Some days he even tried his hand at cooking. Neither of them actually mentioned the subject of role reversal but that is what actually had happened. Not only that but Elise found herself falling in love with the man she had married.

Soon Elise had so much work to do that she advertised for an assistant. It had to be someone with as much care and attention to detail as Elise herself had. That meant finding a place for her to work in the house which was alright in the short term but it might upset the local council if they found out. So when a tatty little shop came up in town, Elise wanted to take it. When she broached the subject with Raymond, he was supportive. He knew that this was to be a long commitment but relished it. How he had changed.

Because Elise was a good friend to Penny, Ben and Vic pulled out all the stops to get the little shop fitted out and ready in short order. Vic also introduced her to the secretary of the chamber of commerce and even arranged for her to come to a Rotary Club lunch and address the members about her new business venture. Elise turned out to be a very good businesswoman. When she advertised for assistance, she was approached by all sorts of people, especially young mothers who wanted a bit of part time work for extra money. She carefully recorded all their details and in due course was able to offer them temporary jobs for holiday relief and such like so that she no longer had time to type because she was too busy organising a profitable work force. At home, Raymond flourished and family life was happier than it had ever been.

They had been so busy that they had neglected to acknowledge the help that had come from Penny especially but also Ben, Vic and Mrs Spooner. One Wednesday evening,

Elise brought the subject up with Penny. "Raymond and I would love to ask you and Ben and your parents out for a meal just to show how much we appreciate all that you have done for us."

"What a kind thought," replied Penny, already thinking that whatever happened, they couldn't possibly go to the Majestic again. "They do say that the new Chinese in the High Street is especially good."

"Well, to be honest, Penny, I wouldn't have thought Vic and Mrs Spooner would be into Chinese food but for my part that would be super. Shall we say Saturday week?"

"That will be fine, I'm sure. I'll let them know when I see them tomorrow if you like."

# Chapter Nineteen

As Yorkshire terriers go, he was a classy dog but he really didn't know whether or not he lead a dog's life because he didn't know what a dog's life was.

He lived in a very nice house where every day he was fed bowls of very palatable stuff. There was a large garden for him to run around in and he was never left out in the cold and the rain. Every day, he was taken by car to the municipal park where, on the end of a lead, he almost encountered other dogs by getting close enough to sniff a bum or two if he was quick, or even to enjoy the sensation of having his own bum sniffed now and again.

On the down side, he was put into a bath of perfumed water once a week and then dried with a blast of hot air. Every morning, he was brushed and fluffed up which wasn't all that bad until they put a ridiculous blue ribbon on top of his head like a top knot.

On balance, the good bits outweighed the bad bits, even so there were times when he felt that he ought really to be going down holes after rats and rabbits, whatever they were, but he wasn't sure why. When the bald-headed old man next door took his grotty shed down, he left a hole in the fence, not a big hole but just about big enough for him to get through if he struggled. So he tried. He caught his top knot on a twig and pulled until his eyes watered then suddenly, he was free but the stupid thing had come off and he gladly left it hanging on the hedge, clearly marking the point at which he had escaped.

Now for the rats and rabbits.

# Chapter Twenty

Penny, having let her parents in for a Chinese meal without checking first, began to wonder at her wisdom. There was no doubt that her mother wouldn't want to go to the Majestic but father had a much thicker skin and wouldn't realise that anything might be amiss. But mentioning the Chinese restaurant had been a reaction without thought and she really had no idea whether or not they liked the stuff. After work next day, they were all sitting in the front room with a cup of tea when Penny told them that they had all been invited for a Chinese meal.

"Chinese?" said Vic in astonishment. "Did you say Chinese?"

"Well, er yes, actually," said Penny lamely.

"Didn't you say that your mother and I don't care for it?"

"Well, no. You see it was on the spur of the moment. It was me who suggested it before they mentioned the Majestic."

"What's wrong with the Majestic?"

"Nothing. It's just that I thought…" Penny trailed off.

Mrs Spooner understood only too well so she intervened. "That sounds to me like a refreshing change. I think we shall all enjoy it."

"What! Chopsticks and all," said Vic.

"Of course, chopsticks and all. We've got over a week to practise and we can start right now."

So that evening they walked up to the Chinese take-away opposite the football ground and peered uselessly at the menu in the window.

"What shall we have?" asked Vic.

"I don't know but we must start somewhere." They followed a young couple into the shop and eavesdropped their conversation.

"Feast number four for five and two number twenty twos please?"

Mrs Spooner looked at Vic and shrugged. They waited while the couple were served a mountain of cartons and left.

"What you rike, Sir?" asked the little Chinaman with a huge smile.

"I've no idea really," said Vic. "So let's take a chance and try a Ling Ho special."

"Ah! Number eleven," said the Chinaman.

"Yes, and sweet and sour pork balls as well."

"Number twenty-two," said the proprietor with a smile.

"That's all," said Vic.

"You want lice with that?"

Mrs Spooner pulled a face but Vic knew instantly what he meant. "Yes please. Ordinary rice."

"Will be five minutes. Please wait."

He disappeared out the back. Vic looked at his wife and said, "I wonder if all the Chinese eat like this."

"How do you mean?"

"Well, does he come home from work and say, 'What's for tea darling,' and she says, 'Twenty-two and chips'?"

"Don't be daft."

They took their meal home and tried it, with chopsticks. They enjoyed the sweet and sour pork but the Ling Ho special tasted like cooked earth and looked even worse.

"What do you think of the rice?" asked Vic.

"It's a bit bland. I think I'll try the rice noodles tomorrow."

Over the next ten days, they went through the menu fairly extensively in preparation for Chinese Saturday and carefully listed the names of the relatively few items that they found enjoyable. These were carefully memorised so that, come the day, they would be able to choose and enjoy without embarrassment. They didn't let Penny and Ben know what they had been up to for fear of making them anxious.

As it turned out, Saturday was a dreadful day with high winds and bouts of heavy rainfall, just the sort of evening when you would like to curl up by the fire with a Chinese take-away. Vic and Mrs Spooner had arranged to stay over at Penny's that night so they all set off for the restaurant together in Elise's people carrier. The restaurant had a porch with inner and outer doors to protect the customers from the weather, even so, with six of them all hurrying in to get out of the rain, both doors were open at the same time, albeit briefly, so the floor was a bit wet inside.

They took off their coats which were taken off to somewhere in the back then sat with a drink and a menu which would take half an hour to read. Worse than that, the things listed were totally different to anything listed at the take-away. Vic gave his wife a look and a shrug and she did the same back. So they sat there bewildered and were grateful when Elise suggested that they should have feast number seven for six because it had such a variety to choose from. They agreed more or less by default.

They were shown to a table next to a group of eight young people, four of each gender, obviously out for a good time. Vic. had to squeeze in sideways past a young lady who looked and smelled as if she had just got out of the bath. She was cracking on about a hairdresser called Andre who had charged only forty-five quid to create the hairstyle which gave her the appearance of having just got out of the bath. They were soon settled comfortably at a circular table with a revolving bit in the middle but Vic and Mrs Spooner were both anxious because they felt sure that they would soon be making fools of themselves or causing embarrassment to their hosts.

The thin Chinese waiter was serving the young people on the next table as another party of eight, having finished their meal and put their coats on, started to leave. Inevitably, the inner and outer doors were open briefly at the same moment, which was just enough for a poor, tired, soaking wet Yorkshire terrier to slip into the warm inviting interior and make a bee-line for the one place he knew where he wouldn't be trodden upon. Under a table. Once there, he decided, as dogs do, to shake off the surplus moisture. Miss Just-out-of-the-Bath got the full force of the icy water all over her legs and gave a scream. She bent below the table and came up to say, "It's a dog," but she didn't get the words out of her mouth because she popped up right underneath a tray containing the ingredients for aromatic duck. The tray went flying and the contents too. Unfortunately, the dish of plum sauce landed on top of Andre's creation which brought yet another scream from the same source. The dog, sensing retribution of some kind, had the good sense to move to another table. It was Raymond who bent down, laid the pink damask table napkin over it to keep his hands clean, then picked it up a put it on his lap.

The Chinese waiter looked at the mess then looked at the dog and screamed at Raymond. "You can't bring dog in restaurant."

"I didn't. I found it under the table."

"Give it to me. I throw it out."

"No."

"Why not?"

"I'll not see a dog thrown out on a night like this."

"It's only a dog."

In the meantime, of course, Miss Just-out-of-the-Bath was yelling blue murder, not at the dog but at the waiter who was trying to get the dog thrown out.

"It's not the dog's fault, it's you, you clumsy Chinaman," or words to that effect.

"Dog must go out," he insisted. The manager had now joined him and also said that the dog must go. "Well, in that case," said Raymond, "I'm going too."

To Vic and Mrs Spooner, this was a heaven-sent opportunity. "That goes for us as well." And they both stood up in solidarity with Raymond. By now, everyone in the restaurant had taken one side or the other and pandemonium reigned as they were all calling out their support or otherwise. Next Elise stood up, then Penny and Ben, all demanding coats. Raymond had the sudden inspiration of seeing who the dog belonged to. He read from the tag, "His name's Lucky and his owner is called Carruthers." Nobody could have begun to understand why this made Vic and his family laugh so much. Even Raymond and Elise looked at them as if they were barmy as they filed out into the wind and rain, hungry and unfed.

They all piled into the people carrier, grateful to be out of the awful weather. As they settled down for the ride home, Ben produced from somewhere a portion of duck done to a crisp. "Look Lucky. I found this on the floor. I'm sure they don't want it."

Once indoors at Raymond and Elise's house, Vic called up the Carruthers' on the phone. "Hello Mrs Carruthers. Vic Spooner here. Have you by any chance lost a dog?"

"Yes," she sounded excited. "How did you know? Have you found him?"

"He's safe and well and currently chewing on a piece of overdone duck," he replied. "If you'd like to come and get him, we are at Penny and Ben's next door neighbour's house. But there's a ransom to pay."

"I was thinking of posting a reward of £100. Will that do?"

"Far too much. All you have to do is go to the Chinese take-away opposite the football ground and get six number sixteens, three number twelves and three number twenty twos."

"Will you want any rice with that?" she enquired.

"Yes please. Oh! And see if he's got nice roodles, will you."

"I'll do no such thing."

As Vic turned away from the telephone joining in with the laughter at his own mistake, his right knee gave way and he stumbled against an armchair. Mrs Spooner was beside him in a flash. "What's up?" she asked.

"It's the third time that damned knee has let me down. I suppose it's years of climbing and crawling about creeping up on me," he explained.

"Well then, it's off to the doctor for you in the morning."

# Chapter Twenty-One

The doctor took little time to determine that Vic needed something serious doing to his knee so he was referred to an orthopaedic surgeon at the local hospital. He had to wait for about three months before the appointment so took to using a walking stick which impaired his ability as a builder but Ben was very supportive and took the load off Vic's shoulders. By the time he attended the hospital, Vic was in severe pain nearly all the time and regularly taking pain killers at night. The surgeon looked at the X-rays and asked Vic to walk up and down the consulting room. Then he was up on the bed having the knee joint pulled almost from its socket. "You need a new knee joint," he declared.

Vic thought that a bit severe. "Can't you do anything with injections or anything?" he asked, not caring at all for the prospect of major surgery.

"No. The whole thing is worn out. Look." And he pointed out to Vic on the X-ray plate what was only too obvious even to an amateur. "If you want it done, I can put you on a list, then you wait for as long as it takes."

"Is that it then?" asked Vic.

"No, there's more to it than that. First you will have to sign a consent form. You can't do that until I have explained to you that there are risks."

"What risks?"

"Well, for starters, I would estimate that about one patient in ten is less than satisfied with the result of this type of surgery."

Vic said that he thought that about one person in ten was less than satisfied with everything.

"You may be right at that." The surgeon continued. "Then there is the matter of the anaesthetic. For a man of your age, I would say that there is a chance of around one in a hundred and fifty that you won't survive it."

"But surely, I'll not know if I don't survive it," queried Vic. "Just so."

"Is there anything else I should know?" Vic was getting a little diffident now.

"Yes. The physiotherapy afterwards will make your eyes water a bit but you still have plenty of muscle there so I would expect your recovery to be quicker than average."

Vic went outside and related this to his wife all except the statistic about dying under anaesthetic. She helped Vic to decide to do what he knew he would have to do so he went back and signed the consent form.

The members of the Rotary Club had become accustomed to seeing Vic with a walking stick by the time he got the call. For Vic's part, he had become accustomed to it himself and had let the importance of the forthcoming operation slip to the back of his mind. So when he was suddenly required to attend for a pre-admission medical in three days' time, it all started to work on his mind. It wasn't what you would call fear but trepidation. Every waking moment he started to think about the one in ten who turned out to be less than satisfied with the surgery and whether he might finish up with something worse than he had at present or how his wife would feel if he failed to come round. He could usually dismiss these thoughts except in the wee hours of the morning when rationality was ever elusive. Within seven days of the pre-admission check, he was admitted to a mixed ward of four ladies and two gentlemen. Some were hips and some were knees.

There was little time to get to know any of them. Some, like Vic, were listed for surgery in the morning and others had been operated upon that day and were still recovering from the effects of the anaesthetic. He had little chance to check the food because he was on 'nil by mouth' right from the start. He passed a restless night wondering what the following day would bring. He didn't know it but all the others on the list were thinking similar thoughts. He lay there listening to his heartbeat. He knew his blood pressure was high because he heard every pulse through the bones behind his ears. He even detected the irregularity, the missed beat, the heavy beat. He wondered whether the ECG had been at fault, or even if he had developed a heart condition in the week since it was done. He finally slept and woke in time to be taken down.

The good thing about anaesthesia is the totality of the oblivion. When he came round, he wasn't even aware that time had passed until gradually it came to him that he could now be counted as the one in one hundred and forty-nine who survived and for that he offered up a little prayer of thanks. He was connected to the hospital equipment in several ways. A tube over his shoulder and across his face gave an enrichment of oxygen to his breathing. From the middle of his back, there was a tube attached to a suspended device which automatically fed something called epidural to kill pain. From above the wound, there were two drainage tubes leading to bottles by the bedside and of course a catheter. As soon as he was aware of anything, a nurse was testing the feeling, or lack of it, in his lower body by placing a lump of ice on his waist, hips and feet. And he didn't half fancy a cup of tea.

Mrs Spooner visited that evening and was pleased to see him awake and well. Although they had not openly discussed the statistics of anaesthetic mortality, they had both been aware of the danger and both were relieved. Later he discussed the matter with the other patients on the ward and found that they had all suffered the same misgivings for the same reasons, and upon waking enjoyed the same relief at having dodged the grim reaper.

On the day following surgery, a nurse brought water and washed his back then left him to wash himself where he could reach. Then he was subjected to the funny puzzle of getting out of the gown, which had ties across his back, and into pyjamas. Not at all difficult until you take into account the tubes from all over his body and working out which sleeve, leg or other gap they could be fed through in order to continue to kill pain, drain wounds and dispose of urine without causing the patient to fall over. That was necessary because two young lady physiotherapists came to get him up. They assured him that, even so soon after surgery, he would be able to carry his full weight on the repaired leg provided he kept the knee straight. He had no intention of bending it. He couldn't. Once in a chair, he was encouraged to walk with the aid of a frame every now and again and to do gentle press ups against a wall. Then he had to lie flat and raise the repaired leg twenty times per session. Then he got to bending exercises and within a short time, he found that he was making progress.

It was only a matter of days before the surgeon signed him off and he was told by the physio that he would be put to the stair test on the following day. Once you pass the stair test, you can go home. Penny and Ben were visiting when he got that news. He had been told that occupational therapy would be coming up to see him and they arrived during Penny and Ben's visit. He was persuaded to purchase at low cost a long-handled shoe horn and a long arm reacher which enabled him to pick things off the floor without bending down. They also said that Vic would need something for the lavatory. It was a sort of frame which converted an ordinary W.C. into something like a throne with arms to give support. This was an appliance loaned by the local authority for the necessary recovery period and was delivered from a depot somewhere by social services. They needed information about the address for delivery, when somebody would be home and so forth so Ben volunteered to go down to reception to make the arrangements. Elsie Mann happened to be on duty. She didn't recognise Ben, just asked him to complete the appropriate form. Ben wrote the address and other details on the form and handed it back. Elsie only glanced at the form as Ben took his leave. When he was gone, she looked at the form in order to take some action and realised that she had seen that strange writing before – on a package containing £5000.

After ten days at home during which Vic undertook his exercises meticulously, he was due to return to the hospital for a proper physiotherapy session in the gym. If he had thought the exercises so far had been hard, he was yet to discover the pain of standing on a step and bending the new joint so as to lower his entire weight to the ground then to lift it back up again. He reported to reception where he was greeted by Elsie Mann.

"Mr Spooner. You may not remember me but I am Elsie Mann. You will be in the charge of Miss Collins. Before you go into the gym, would you mind telling me who it was that filled in the forms for your WC accessories?"

"That would have been Ben, my son-in-law. Why, is anything wrong?"

"No, nothing is wrong but I do need to see him."

"Is it a matter of business?"

"No. Anyway it's not hospital business, it's a private matter that I need to see him about." This got Vic worried.

"What's he done then?"

"Look, I can't really talk about it here. I finish at four. Would you mind seeing me in the refectory after Miss Collins has finished with you?"

"If I'm still standing. They said on the ward that she was hard as nails."

"I don't know about that," replied Elsie, "but she's very pretty."

And with that a most attractive and feminine young lady came to collect Vic and put him through it.

When Vic finished, he wandered down to the refectory wondering what on earth awaited him. He hoped that Ben hadn't got into any trouble although he thought that highly unlikely. He found Elsie sitting there with Mrs Spooner who had come to drive Vic home. "Hello, you two," he began, "of course you know each other from WI I suppose."

Mrs Spooner asked Vic how the session had gone and he gave a non-helpful reply. Elsie Mann offered to buy them both a cup of tea. Vic declined. "Not here," he said, "I don't care for these colystyrene pups. Let's go over the road to the tea rooms."

They did so and as the three of them settled into a corner where they could talk, Elsie told them why she wanted to speak to Ben. "I hope I'm not breaking any confidences here but I have reason to think that your Ben donated £5000 to the church some years ago. Am I right?"

Mrs Spooner's mind was racing ahead. "You could be. Why do you ask?"

"Because he wrote something on the package and I have only just been able to identify the writing."

"But what has that to do with you?" asked Mrs Spooner.

"I made a terrible mistake over that money. I took it and used it for myself, believing it to have been a gift to me. Then about two years back, someone in this town was very kind to me and replaced some money that I had lost due to the sudden death of an old friend. That was when I knew of my error and it has been haunting me ever since."

"There's a lot more to this than meets the eye," said Mrs Spooner. "I think it would be a good idea for you to meet Ben and explain things otherwise you'll never get rid of your guilty feelings. Would you like me to arrange it?"

"Oh, yes please, Wendy."

# Chapter Twenty-Two

Mrs Spooner was quite a perceptive woman at times. She lay in bed thinking about the meeting with Elsie Mann and soon put two and two together. Before she slept, she had decided that the meeting would take place in that new Italian spaghetti and pizza place which had been getting some good reports in the paper. She also decided that the Rev Theodore Thornthwaite should be present but Elsie must not know that in advance. Next morning, she telephoned and made a booking for six people. By a strange coincidence, John Carruthers also telephoned to make a booking for two.

Mrs Spooner arranged that Elsie would call to pick up her and Vic and that Penny would drive Ben and pick up Theodore on the way. She was forbidden to say that Elsie Mann would be there, he would find out when it was too late for him to run away from her yet again. She had chosen the Italian place for a number of reasons. First, it had good reviews, then it was nicely positioned in a suburb still referred to as the village, then it was a pleasant run out and a pretty setting opposite a duck pond. The proprietors had had a lot of trouble getting planning permission for use as a restaurant because it was an old timber schoolhouse grade two listed. It had been necessary for the front to be left unchanged to preserve the village character of the area. The playground made a splendid car park round the back and the main entrance was through the old green door with only one very discreet sign to indicate the commercial activity within. Once inside the gabled porch, there was a door on the left leading to the lavatories and a large green cupboard on the right which some of the older inhabitants remembered from their schooldays. The lobby extended another twelve feet or more where once the walls were lined with a bench each side and rows of coat hooks. These were all gone now and replaced by the essentials of this sort of building. At the back of the lobby, double swing doors led into the restaurant proper and what a difference there was then. A suspended ceiling concealed the old roof trusses and match boarding of the old structure and the rectangular shape was broken up cleverly by trellised partitions with climbing plants and a curved bar with comfortable seating. It looked very inviting. The manager dressed in white shirt and red bow tie made a point of welcoming in every diner. He was a fussy little individual who wore an impressive bunch of keys hanging from a loop at his trouser belt.

Penny, Ben and Theodore arrived first, by careful arrangement, and took the reserved table. Vic, Elsie and Mrs Spooner arrived soon afterwards. When Elsie saw Theo, she almost stopped in her tracks but Mrs Spooner was ready for the reaction and more or less pushed her forward. Theo, ever the complete gentleman, stood up at Elsie's approach and as she sat down, he said how pleased he was to see her again after such a long time. They ordered drinks and food. Elsie and Theo were clearly ill at ease so Mrs Spooner began.

"The reason why this meeting has been arranged is to enable Elsie to explain to Ben why his so-called anonymous donation to the church roof fund was misappropriated by mistake." The others looked on wondering what was coming next. "Well, it's about time we all laid our cards on the table and since that will be very hard for some of those present, I propose to tell it as I think it is. Please stop me if I go wrong." Mrs Spooner then proceeded to relate the entire saga starting with young Ben's robbery. She made shrewd assumptions about the reasons why Elsie had assumed the money left in the church had been a personal gift from Theo and although both looked a little embarrassed at this, neither tried to stop her. When she made reference to the benefactor who chose to replace Elsie's lost money, it caused the latter's eyebrows to go up as it dawned on her who the benefactor had been. At the end of her address, which had taken a full twenty minutes to deliver allowing for the interruption of food being served, Mrs Spooner looked at them all and said, "Have I understood everything correctly, including Elsie's feelings for you Theo and," looking directly at Theo, "your innate fear of expressing personal feelings of any tender sort.?"

Elsie and Theo both looked partly taken aback and partly embarrassed but neither could refute a word of what Mrs Spooner had said.

"Then I think it is high time that you two put this all behind you so that Elsie can get back to attending church and cleaning the brass as I know she loves to do."

That was it. Mrs Spooner had hit the nail on the head, done the whole embarrassing thing for Elsie better than she could ever have done for herself.

Vic had sat in silent wonder as his wife had taken the floor to resolve such a difficult problem so easily but it hadn't stopped him from having a couple so he really needed to leave the table. He left his walking stick and used his hand to hang on to chair backs and things as he made his way towards the lobby doors. For the last three yards of his walk, there were no chair backs so he strode forward across the gap with confidence and placed a firm steadying hand on one of the big brass handles. It so happened that at the same moment, John Carruthers placed a firm hand on the big brass handle on the other side of the door. Whereas Vic was trying to maintain his balance, Carruthers was bent on sweeping the door towards him in a magnificent gesture to allow his wife to enter. The force of Carruthers' pull yanked Vic forward and propelled him into the opening as Mrs Carruthers stepped forward. As Vic pitched forward, he grasped her round the waist in a sort of rugby tackle and they both went down with the lady ending up in a sitting position with her back against the green cupboard and Vic's head cradled in her lap. Carruthers exploded, "Spooner. What the hell do you think you're doing assaulting my wife." And he leaned forward to grasp Vic by the shoulder.

"Oh John. Don't be so silly. You know he's only just out of hospital." Mrs Carruthers wasn't anxious for Vic to get up. She found it quite pleasant cradling his head thus.

Her husband remembered that he had been told at Rotary that Vic had had surgery and immediately regretted his outburst. "Look here, sorry old chap. I quite forgot."

The manager as ever on duty just inside the swing door hurried out. "Oh dear. Are you hurt, sir?"

"No. I'm fine, thanks but I'll stay here for a minute or so to get my breath back." He too was comfortable in the lady's lap.

Eventually the two men together bent down one each side to lift Vic to his feet. As they did so, the keys on the manager's belt caught on the fire extinguisher on the wall. Vic was expecting to be dropped as they all held their breath while it rolled harmlessly to the floor. Vic then took himself off to the toilet as Mrs Spooner came into the lobby with Vic's walking stick. "Hello Joan. What are you doing on the floor?"

"Don't ask, dear. It's too complicated to explain."

The manager turned to pick up the fire extinguisher as Mrs Spooner looked at it wondering why it was in the middle of the floor. He picked it up by what appeared to be the handle but with the safety pin and pull ring still hanging from his belt, it was now the trigger. He realised his mistake as soon as he felt the lever depress and crush the actifying glass phial inside. But he was quick to react. As the rubber hose began to rise under water pressure, he grabbed it and steered the jet of water away from the two ladies, aiming it up towards the ceiling, across the top of the cupboard towards the door. Carruthers was equally quick and opened the outer door so that the manager stepped smartly outside where the appliance emptied itself harmlessly onto the grass.

Vic emerged from the toilet and the five of them started back to the restaurant laughing about their lucky escape and praising the manger for his swift reactions. As the inner door opened, the water from the ceiling seeped through the top of the green cupboard, dripped onto the electricity consumer unit and with a considerable bang, the whole place was plunged into total darkness. There were various reactions. Some cheered, some screamed and some laughed but Theodore and Elsie did none of these things. In the darkness they each reached out their hands toward each other. Theo had never before reached a hand towards Elsie because he had been afraid to. Now, as he sat opposite her in the darkness, he found that he enjoyed the experience in a way that he would not have thought possible.

It was only a matter of moments before the emergency fire escape lighting kicked in. It bathed the diners in a dim bluish light, just enough to see the fire exits and get to them without falling over. Mrs Spooner looked across at Theo and Elsie, two mature and sensible people, holding hands across the table like a couple of teenagers. Penny and Ben saw them too, quietly excused themselves and came across to join her parents in the doorway. "Mother," she began with mock severity. "I never had you down as a matchmaker."

Mrs Spooner smiled. "I think we had better go home now, don't you?"

Vic interrupted, "Not until I've had my ice cream." And he set off towards the table. Mrs Spooner grabbed his arm and restrained him. "Look, you idiot. Do you think they could look any happier if they were sitting on a bench by the public toilets with steaming mugs and bacon sandwiches?"

Vic remembered the moment. "Yes, I see what you mean. We'll have ice cream at home, shall we?"

# Chapter Twenty-Three

Three weeks passed before Theodore came to a Rotary Club meeting and the singing of grace was discordant without his piano playing. When he did return, he was greeted with smiles all round because all and sundry had heard of the events at the Italian restaurant and some versions had been embellished. Vic was especially pleased to see him for the right reasons and immediately bought him a drink. When the initial welcoming had died down a bit, he motioned Vic to a quiet corner where they could talk without interruption.

"The thing is," he began, "that Elsie and I have, er, shall we say, formed an emotional attachment."

"Well, that's a surprise," replied Vic a little facetiously.

"Yes. And I rather hoped that you..." He trailed off as the bell went for lunch so Vic had to wait for three quarters of an hour before he got the rest of the sentence.

"The thing is, we've decided to marry."

"Well, I'll be damned," said Vic irreverently. "We thought you'd never get round to it."

"Well, we have, and because of the part that you and your wife played in bringing us together, I would deem it an honour if you would be my best man."

"And I would deem it a privilege to accept," an excited Vic spluttered out in reply.

When Vic got home, Mrs Spooner was still at her WI meeting and he was impatient to tell her his news. When she came in, he burst out with, "Guess what?"

"Elsie Mann and Theodore Thornthwaite are getting married," she said all matter-of-factly.

"Oh, I suppose Elsie has told everyone, has she?"

"Well, of course, she would hardly keep good news like that a secret, would she?"

"I suppose not. But you don't know the best bit."

"Don't tell me she's pregnant."

"Don't be disgusting. No – Theodore wants me to be his best man."

"Oh Lord. You haven't accepted, have you?"

"Yes, of course I have. Why shouldn't I?"

"You will have to make a speech, that's why not. You know what you are like when you get excited. You get your words all muddled up and I would hate to see you make a fool of yourself."

Vic was quiet for a moment. Then he said, "I know I have that problem and I would really like to show everyone that I can overcome it. I'm about due to be president of the Rotary Club but I can't see me getting elected unless I can show them that I can make a speech properly when I put my mind to it."

"Very well then," his wife replied. "Put your mind to it and I'll be rooting for you all the time. By the way, did you ask who will be officiating. Theo can hardly marry himself, can he?"

"No, I suppose not. I didn't think to ask."

"Well, Elsie told us all at WI. You will be delighted to hear that the bishop is coming down to do the service, and for good measure, he's staying for the wedding breakfast."

"Oh dear," was Vic's inadequate response.

Members of Rotary met to consider what they should buy for a wedding present. What they wondered about was what to get for a couple who each had a home full of equipment. They would have two of everything already. It was Willy Sidebottom who came up with the brilliant idea of providing a wedding reception. They agreed that as most of them would be there anyway, it would be a bit like buying their own supper but when it was put to Theodore, he was in agreement because it would save him the trouble of organising it. The ladies of the WI had a similar meeting and decided to provide a wedding cake.

Phil Collins said he would lay on the reception at the golf club. The cost would be reasonable and the standard very good. Not only that but his daughter Amanda was at university and was forever looking for work between terms. The club would need extra staff so he would get her a job waiting at table.

The arrangements were all made and the big day arrived. Theo and Elsie had few relations but the turnout from WI, the church and Rotary was very considerable. It has to be said that an actual bishop in all his finery added something magnificent to the occasion and he carried it off with dignity and sincerity. When the service was over, a considerable motorcade proceeded to the golf club for the meal. The tables were set out beautifully with a top table and three sprigs and the staff were all on their toes. Amanda had been given the job of wine waiter because she said that she had done it before. They all took their places with the bride and groom, best man, bishop and others of importance in Rotary or the church. As it happened, they were all experienced top tablers. At most official functions, it is the practice that the hoi polloi on the sprigs buy their own wine so no question arises about how much they drink. After all, if you pay for it, you can drink as much or as little as you choose. On the top table however, the wine is usually provided by the host so that each top tabler has to struggle with his conscience whenever the wine waiter asks, "More wine, Sir?" So top tablers have worked out a system of imbibing well without appearing to do so. If your attention is diverted when the wine waiter comes along, he will not interrupt you to ask if you need a top up, he'll just do it.

So the top tablers have developed a skill. What you do is keep a weather eye open for the wine waiter and as he approaches, take a long draught of wine then engage the person on your left in intense conversation. The wine waiter arrives at your right shoulder and politely does not interrupt your conversation. As soon as you have been topped up, you turn to the person on your right whilst your erstwhile conversationalist engages the person on his left and so on down the table. Seen from the front this technique has a slow but definite rhythm to it. It hasn't the magnificence of a Mexican wave, more like a Surbiton ripple.

The bishop enjoyed his wine and had discovered over the years that by adopting this procedure, he imbibed just enough to make him happy and not quite enough to make him stupid. But he hadn't reckoned with Amanda. She thought it would be good sport to get the bishop tiddly. Her father, being a prominent member of the National Association of Estate

Agents, was an expert top tabler himself and had told Amanda about this trick and how to pace things. But left to her own devices, Amanda thought she could easily fit in a couple of extra visits and make sure the bishop had a very full measure each time. She reckoned that she could induce him into taking at least two glasses more than he usually had. That would be something to talk about back at university.

And that is exactly what she set out to do.

At the end of the meal, Vic rose to make his speech. To say that many of those present were on tenterhooks would be to understate the case. Some less well-inclined towards Vic were actually waiting for a chance to guffaw as soon as he slipped up as he surely would. But, wonder of wonders, he didn't. He had practised so hard and learned his speech so well that he was word perfect. He managed to say "rightful feelings" without turning it into "frightful reelings." He referred to "days of hope" without calling them "haze of dope" and best of all he spoke of a "meeting of souls" without saying "seating of moles". It was a fine address well delivered and when he had finished, there was applause. It wasn't merely the polite applause following a best man speech, it was more than that. His friends and family were acknowledging a job well done as well. Vic soon recognised that the applause was too loud and too long so he stood again with a glass held aloft in his left hand and his right hand with palm turned towards the reception to quieten them just as a celebrity would do. He was milking the moment while it lasted. Finally, when the applause had died down, Vic said, "Ladies and Gentlemen. Please be upstanding and glaze your arses in toast."

There was a shocked silence at this embarrassing gaffe, or at least the beginning of a shocked silence because the tipsy bishop stood up and said loudly, "The Gride and Broom." Then he took a long draught of wine, sat down heavily and slumped forward into the wedding cake.

On the way home, Mrs Spooner said, "It was a shame about the wedding cake."

"Yes. Do you fancy a bacon sandwich?"

"Why not." And they wandered off to find the public lavatories.

**THE END**

CPSIA information can be obtained
at www.ICGtesting.com
Printed in the USA
BVHW010632260321
603454BV00003B/32

9 781788 238229